Tales of a Wanderer
A Journey's Start

BY STEFAN AZIMIOARA

The contents of this work, including, but not limited to, the accuracy of events, people, and places depicted; opinions expressed; permission to use previously published materials included; and any advice given or actions advocated are solely the responsibility of the author, who assumes all liability for said work and indemnifies the publisher against any claims stemming from publication of the work.

Dorrance Publishing Co
585 Alpha Drive
Pittsburgh, PA 15238
Visit our website at *www.dorrancebookstore.com*

ISBN: 978-1-6853-7070-1
ESIBN: 978-1-6853-7917-9

Tales of a Wanderer
A Journey's Start

I've spent a lot of lonely nights with only some music and my thoughts for company, and this is a story I've thought about for some time now. From time to time, I get lost in my own world, just thinking to myself. I've decided to write it down, simply because I want to.

Chapter One
Fire in the Snow

FOOTSTEPS IN THE SNOW.
That's about the only thing you could see for a few miles besides the blankets of white. Snowfall was light, but just enough to cover the tracks made by a man in a tattered cloak. In his bag, he held enough food and supplies to last him a couple days and, on his back, he carried a metallic staff. Checking his map, he muttered the name of a close by town.

"Kupai," he said and took out his compass. After realizing that it wasn't working, he gave it a few angry taps and put it away. Continuing his journey, he passed over another dune of snow and finally found the town.

It was in shambles. Fire was set upon all the wooden buildings and was able to burn easily despite the snow. As soon as he neared the remnants of the village the stranger started finding the residents of Kupai, who were face down on the ground. None were moving. He stepped over the fresh corpses and trekked through the pools of blood making his way into town.

At first thinking the cause of this disaster to be the mess left behind by a large group of bandits, he stopped upon noticing the hilt of a broken knife partially hidden under a broken wheelbarrow. It appeared to belong to the corpse of an older man, who looked like he suffered more slash wounds than the rest of the villagers, and what's more was that his body appeared to be dragged to where he lay. The stranger followed the marks on the ground left behind by this man to the closest house.

Among the ruins of the house, there were bits of broken furniture and glass that were not caused by fire damage, and among them, a piece of armor that had a symbol of a blue dragon. The man was convinced that this wasn't just some bandit raid anymore, even if all the valuables were missing. He pocketed the shard of armor. Searching throughout the house, he could find nothing more and was about to leave when he tripped on plank revealing another body hidden in the floorboards, this time of a girl. After a closer inspection, he realized she was still breathing, but had a sprained ankle and a large gash on her forehead. The man in the cloak wasted no more time and took her away from the burning building.

Chapter Two
Introductions

REVINA LOOKED OUTSIDE A SMALL CRACK IN THE BOARDED-up window in her home. Outside, there was madness. Fires were being set on the neighbor's houses by archers with flaming arrows, and soldiers in armor were breaking down doors, dragging out screaming people and executing them on the spot. Her father pulled her away from the window and led her to some removed floorboards in the middle of the room.

"Now . . . Revina—" her father started.

"No!" she sobbed.

"Revina. This has to happen. Whatever you do, do not make a sound." Revina's father hugged his daughter one last time and then laid her down in the hole on the floor.

He set to work, quickly placing boards on top of Revina until she was completely covered. It was just in time too, as the soldiers and the screaming that accompanied them, made their way to his front door. The man took a small knife from the kitchen table and hid behind the front door. There was a loud banging, then the door broke open with the first of the soldiers pouring in. Revina's father plunged his blade into the shoulder of the first trooper, which shattered upon impact against the infantryman's armor. The blade broke apart, as did a piece of the soldier's armor. Furious, the

3

soldier pierced his ambusher straight through with his sword. Blood flowed down the already dead man, through the cracks in the floorboards onto Revina's horrified face. Her father's blood mixed with her tears and stung her eyes. She started to scream, but thankfully the terror robbed all noise from her voice.

As the soldier dragged Revina's father outside, the infantry behind him moved into the house, looting, breaking, and pillaging everything in sight. They were angry, apparently not finding what they wanted. Each person was cursing. Blood-soaked, Revina did her best to cry silently. After they finished, the soldiers lit torches and tossed them into the house setting the place ablaze. The men left the home, and before the outside air was full of screams, but now there was terrible silence.

Revina couldn't contain herself anymore and cried aloud. As she cried, the fire got worse and worse, spreading from the walls to the ceiling, and weakening the building. This whole experience was too much for her to handle, and the same went for the ceiling. The roof collapsed inward, directly on top of the floorboards which hid Revina, knocking her unconscious.

⁓

Revina awoke to find herself bandaged and wrapped in a blanket. She leaned against a small cave wall listening to the soft crackling of a campfire.

"Eat," interrupted a stranger, who was sitting on the other side of the fire. It was then when she noticed a bowl of soup at her feet, still warm with foreign vegetables.

"Who are you?" she asked before taking a sip.

"Eat," he simply replied.

"Is that your name? Eat?" Revina responded, annoyed.

The man sighed, "Call me Frank. Now please eat."

Revina drank some soup and then put it back down and stared at it for a while. "Everyone's dead, aren't they?"

"Not true, you are still alive," he responded.

Revina continued to stare at her soup.

"Then what? What am I supposed to do?" she asked helplessly

"That's up for you to decide, but as long as you're in my care, you will be safe."

Revina stared at her soup some more.

"I plan to move back south and get out of this weather. You are welcome to leave if you want. I'll leave you part of my provisions." He took out from his bag a large gold purse with almost a hundred gold pieces. "I'll leave you with this, so you can actually provide for yourself."

Revina stopped staring at her soup. That was more than a year's worth of crops from her father's farm. She had only seen that much money only once before, when a noble came by to her house a few months earlier.

"H-h-how do you have that?" she exclaimed. "Do you just walk around with that much gold in your pockets all the time? There are a lot of bandits who could take it and would definitely attack if they saw that!"

"Well, it's not like I just flaunt it around all the time," he said putting it away. "You know if you can shout at me like that then we should move. Take the blanket, and if we don't want to starve or freeze, I suggest we leave now so we can get ahead of the next storm." Frank put out the fire and stood up.

Revina stood up, ankle feeling better, and the wound on her forehead still bandaged. As they left the cave, Frank frowned and looked at the hills of snow and the endless stretch of snowing clouds in the sky. He stopped still and was about to take out his broken compass when he remembered that it was useless.

"What?" Revina said.

"I don't know which way is south."

"You can't be serious." Then, looking at his frown, she pointed at a cliff. "That way should lead to Yostel, the next village over."

"Well, then off to Yostel we go." Frank started leading the way despite not necessarily knowing where he was going.

"Some savior. More like a tourist . . ." Revina muttered behind him.

Frank gave her a look and opened his mouth as if he was about to say something, then thought against it.

They left the remains of Kupai behind them and began hiking up long stretches of mountains that would lead them to another town. Revina was amazed. She had never really left the village before. The sun was starting to break through the snow and shone on the mountaintops and valleys.

"Nice view," Frank said, trying to cheer up his unfortunate companion.

Now he really is just like tourist, Revina thought to herself. But he was right, it was rather nice, hard to imagine she had just witnessed something so awful when she was looking at such a breath-taking landscape. She also realized that the path that they were heading through would lead to Yeti's Gorge, the most perilous area near her village.

"We should turn back and go around the mountain," she said.

"Why?"

"The valley up ahead is dangerous."

"And how much time would it take to go around the mountain and get back to the path to Yostel?" Frank asked.

"Five days"

"Well, that's a problem. You see, I didn't really plan on travelling with extra people. I only have enough food to last for one day. So, then we must go down this pass and get to Yostel." Frank paused for a bit, then continued down the mountain.

"But you don't understand—"

"I'd rather take my chances with the yetis rather than the cold," he said.

"Fine." Revina was perplexed. She didn't remember telling the name of the gorge to Frank. She picked up her feet and followed behind him, into the valley.

Chapter Three
Ice and Stone

REVINA KNEW THIS WAS A BAD IDEA. THE TOURIST HAD absolutely no clue what he was doing. Not even soldiers summoned from the King could clear the pass of all the yetis. Despite it being a very remote place, it used to be an important trade route to send food into the Kingdom of Pravah from the southern provinces. That was until the beasts took over the area and slaughtered all those who would wander through, effectively closing the trade route.

It was very deep chasm, a long fall with only darkness beneath them. She assumed the snow below would cushion her fall, but she was not at all eager to try. The large snowy void was spanned by huge natural pillars of ice and stone that were connected by lengthy wooden bridges, that were by now, run down from years of neglect.

"Are you sure about this?" Revina exclaimed over the howling wind.

"Don't tell me you're scared of heights," Frank shouted back.

"I'm more worried about being blown off the mountain!"

Revina looked down the side of the pillar of rock she stood on, and she still couldn't see the bottom. She felt like something was watching them.

"Are you sure about this?" she said.

"You already asked me that."

"Well, you didn't answer!"

"That's cause I'm not sure, not ever." Frank also looked down the pillar. "I did promise to get you to Yostel, so that's what I'll do."

Revina silently followed him to the next massive pillar. What did he mean by he's never sure? It would just be another pillar after the next one, and then they would be out of the gorge. She was wondering why nothing had happened yet. This road was closed because imperial decree deemed it to dangerous, so why did everything look to be so eerily quiet?

And surely enough she looked down again and screamed when she saw them. What looked like five yetis were climbing up the pillars, three on the pillar towards the exit and two on another pillar behind them. They were trapping Frank and Revina on the bridge in between the gap of ice and stone.

"Stories about the mythical beast known as the yeti often describe them as giants, although in reality, they are just as big as a gorilla from a jungle," Frank explained. "However, they are just as dangerous and can easily overpower even men armed with swords. Along with their impressive strength they are quite acrobatic, seeing as they are able to climb up these frozen cliffsides."

Revina just looked at him horrified, "Why are you telling me this?"

"Because that was what I originally came here for, to clear this gorge and slay these beasts. A lot of people told me how this pass was too dangerous and would often leave villages like yours without goods, and trap people like ourselves. Also, I did explain we were short on food, yes? What do you think they're here for?" he said, pointing at the snarling yetis.

"I said we were short on provisions, but another reason why I had us go through this shortcut is because there is nothing we can gain from our surroundings. We can't gather fruit or nuts because all I see is snow and no sustainable wildlife, not even the occasional deer. We'd starve before reaching Yostel."

The yetis were getting nearer, and Revina could see blood stains on their teeth. That means if there's no wildlife around, then those things prey on humans! She clutched her blanket closer, "So draw your weapon! Is that thing on your back just for show? Or are you just going to let them kill us?"

"No that's not necessary," he said. And as one of the yetis in front of them swiped at him with his huge paw, Frank grabbed it, and threw the yeti over Revina, her jaw gaping, and into one of the two yetis on the pillar behind the travelers. This promptly sent both yetis tumbling down the valley.

"No point in killing them if there is no more village this way I suppose," he said.

As the remaining yeti behind Revina watched his friends fall down the mountain, he gave a short roar and charged down the bridge, signifying that the two others in front would do the same. Frank retaliated by jumping over Revina, who could do little more than watch with amazement as Frank used the yeti's face like a springboard, pushed off of the beast while kicking it, and sent himself flying toward the remaining two yetis, which were barreling down the bridge. As they leapt toward him, he kicked both of them in the jaw, sending the yetis hurling off either side of the bridge, while doing a mid-air split.

It became very apparent that the bridge couldn't support all of the movement of three yetis and more on it and collapsed, making Revina lose her footing. Frank quickly grabbed her and made a mad dash towards the pillar. It was too late, and the bridge snapped, but not before Frank could make a jump off the bridge and impaled the next frozen pillar with his metal staff. Strangely enough Revina did not even notice him draw it, and she could've sworn the rock moved slightly, despite being vastly huge and sturdy.

Frank pulled them both over the edge and on top of the pillar and asked, "Are you injured?"

Revina was flabbergasted, despite pulling off stunts like a circus performer and overpowering five huge apes of the frozen tundra, the man in front of her wasn't even out of breath, nor did he seem at all fazed by what just happened.

"Yo-ou-you just . . . how did yo—WHO ARE YOU?" she sputtered.

"I did tell you my name was Frank. Now come on, we've got to get to Yostel, and I don't think we can go back the way we came."

Chapter Four
The City of Yostel

HEY, WHEN YOU SAID THE NEXT VILLAGE WAS OVER THIS way, you did say village, right?" Frank looked at the impressively walled city in the distance. They were out of the cold now, their surroundings were much greener, and pine trees were abundant on the road leading to the city. The two passed a sign that read: "Yostel."

"Well, either way, I supposed our journey here is done." Frank finally took down the hood of his cloak, and Revina was surprised to notice he was young, almost her age. How could someone have that much fighting experience at so young an age?

"Here you go," Frank said as he plopped the bag of gold in her hands. "You can find plenty of people who are willing to help you and take you under their wing here in the city. You could marry or even learn a trade."

"Wait," Revina stopped him. "I want . . . to learn how to fight like you."

"You misunderstand. When I said there would be plenty of people to take you under their wing, I didn't mean myself."

"I don't think anyone in the city could teach me as well as you."

"I think there are people in there who could teach way better. And I never had a student before, doing well in a subject field and teaching it are two different things."

Revina kept insisting until Frank tossed his head back and sighed, "Why do you want to learn from me anyway?" Frank narrowed his eyes at Revina. It was clear that he was expecting a good answer.

"I don't want to be helpless, and I want to stand on my own feet," Revina replied.

"You're doing that right now, and there are plenty of guards around the city who can come to your defense if you get attacked by some ruffian or thug."

"That's not what I meant! I want to be able to protect myself, and there are others out there just like me who will need help too. And I also want to know," Revina's tone started getting serious, "why did my father have to die? And who burned down my village to the ground?"

"So, you want vengeance, is it? To kill the aggressors of your home and family?"

Revina didn't respond. She didn't know what to say to that, because some of it was true. Frank fingered at the broken piece of metal he salvaged earlier in his pocket.

"I'll pay you," Revina said, and with a straight face, handed Frank one hundred gold. "Now teach me."

Frank couldn't help but smile. "Fine," he said, giving up. "I guess I have no choice, but first thing's first." They arrived at the great doors of the city. "We need to get something to eat."

The opening square of the city had a bustle of people moving in and out of shops. Revina was amazed when listening to her father talk about selling vegetables in the town square, but she didn't at all imagine the place would be like this. The cobblestone streets were filled with carriages and merchants selling wares. Shops and services lined every alley. The crowds in the town were great in variety, while there were farmers selling produce, among them were a few adventurers fully clad in armor. There was a musician playing a fiddle somewhere, but Revina couldn't see him. A garrison was tucked away near the city's entrance that had guards stationed around the city like sentries.

"So, this is a city . . ." she said, awestruck.

"Usually taverns are close to the entrance. Let's see if we can find a cheap one with good food," Frank said, spotting a tavern called the Worn-Down Mule. They went inside. Indeed, the place did look worn down and most of the furniture was falling apart. Just as Revina sat down, she found herself on the floor surround by the splinters of what used to be a chair.

"That's coming out of what you order," said a voice from behind a bar counter. It was of an old man, with a grey mustache that was long enough to be a beard. "What're ya havin?" he said while scrubbing a dirty beer glass.

"A pork dinner and two of whatever used to be in that glass, thanks." Frank also added, "And can we get a room for one night please?"

The barkeeper looked at Frank and then at Revina, his long mustache swaying as he did, and winked. "That'll be four silver."

Frank paid him, and the barkeeper went back to fix their drinks and food.

"So, what's the plan?" said Revina, doing her best to avoid eye contact with the barkeeper after getting her drink.

"For now, get some rest. It's been a long day, and tomorrow, we will get more provisions, new clothes, and some weapons. I'm not sure if you're familiar with any of them, but once we have what we need, we'll leave for Ether Woods, where I will train you. You didn't seem to know much of life outside your town, so it will take time to prepare you on how to travel. I guess my profession is more of a mercenary than traveler, so I'll teach you accordingly."

Sure enough, tomorrow, they bought new clothes fit for travel for Revina and an assortment of a sword, spear, bow, shield, and knife. She looked at Frank's tattered cloak and said, "Are you sure you don't want anything?"

"No, quit asking me if I'm sure all the time. Besides, I have a better idea of what to do with the leftover money," he said, stopping at a bookshop. The entrance to the place seemed small on the outside, but the shop's inside had the space of a warehouse. Huge galleries had shelves that held too many books and scrolls for Revina to count.

Behind the counter was another old man that looked eerily similar to the barkeeper. This time, however, the mustache was thin and stood straight up, resembling that of a lobster. "Welcome, you're free to browse until we close."

"You wouldn't happen to have a brother working as a barkeeper by any chance, would you?" Frank asked

"Absolutely not," replied the bookkeeper.

Frank narrowed his eyes in skepticism and left to pick a dozen books off the shelves and hand them to Revina, who couldn't believe her eyes.

"Spell books?" she exclaimed

"Well, of course, didn't you ever get the chance to hear about these in your village before? And it's not just spell books." He stacked on books on plant culture, history, geography, blacksmithing, carpentry, and hunting. "That's all I can think of for now."

After bringing the books to the counter, the bookkeeper squinted his eyes and asked Frank, "Have I met you before?"

"Absolutely not." Frank replied, smiling. "Oh, and we won't take this one," he said, taking one of the spell books out of the pile.

"Very well," said the bookkeeper, and after his customers paid and left, he moved to put the book back by checking the author. Strangely enough, the author looked a lot like the gentleman who just bought those books, though that must've just been a coincidence. At least that's what the bookkeeper thought to himself.

Chapter Five
The Ether Woods

FRANK WAS BESIDE HIMSELF AT THE MOMENT. NEXT TO HIM, Revina eagerly flipped through the spell books as they walked, reading spell names out at random, and asking what each did. They had left Yostel, heading toward the Ether Woods where Frank would train Revina. Frank had no clue how he would teach her anything. He'd never had to teach before, and she also seemed to be very interested in spells, which could prove disastrous.

"I appreciate that you've taken an interest in those writings, but you'll have to put them away for now, we're here."

The two stopped before the entrance to a forest full of trees of all shapes and sizes. It looked like nature's jungle gym. The vegetation had curving branches, and the roots were dug well into the forest's floor making the ground uneven. The foliage grew an abundance of vines that seemed to cover all the trees.

"This forest," explained Frank, "is the perfect place to practice situational awareness. Above all you must have a clear understand of what is happening around you. This may not always be that case as weather might hinder your vision, or a potential threat might try to hide itself and so on." He was doing his best to sound like he knew what he was doing.

"We will train your stamina first. You seemed to do well in

travelling long distances despite being injured. It might be one of your strengths, so let's get to it."

Frank's training was as difficult as Revina expected. She had to run through the forest, keeping up a brisk pace while also moving through not only the treetops and canopies, but also through the twisting grove on the ground. Not to mention the numerous obstacles, such as dead logs and flowers covered in thorns.

"Doing this will also help with your balance," said Frank, watching as Revina fell off another log.

Frustrated, Revina climbed back on the tree, only to fall off of it again.

"Ugh, when will actually train how to fight? I want to be able to protect myself, not be able to run from danger. You haven't even taught me one spell yet!"

Frank sighed, "Look, what I learned was . . . somewhat advanced, okay? That was because I lived *in* danger during my training, and I could've very easily gotten hurt or killed. I'd prefer you not search for trouble, which means being prepared and learning how to avoid combat is the first lesson. Right now, you are weak, meaning you will have to choose your battles wisely."

"All right . . . sorry," Revina mumbled.

They set up a camp and a week passed, and every day was spent the same. They would wake up, find food in the forest, and Revina would train moving around until they went to sleep. Revina got very good at traversing and no longer fell off the trees anymore, but Frank also noticed that she didn't touch the books anymore. She had a passion to learn the spells, and he couldn't help but feel like he shot it down.

"Not today," said Frank as he watched Revina stretching and getting ready for another run around the woods. Frank tossed her a book on basic magic. "We're going to be practicing doing this today. Pick a spell you might want to practice."

Revina looked happily surprised and flipped through the pages, eventually decided on a simple healing spell. "This one," she said, pointing at the book's pages.

"That one?" Frank looked slightly nervous, then calmed down. "All right then, let's try it."

Frank grabbed some thorns off a vine and cut Revina's hand.

"Was there are reason it had to be my hand?" Revina said, wincing as blood was drawn.

"You can't always rely on someone else to heal yourself. Plus, it might not work on me."

Before Revina could question why, Frank quickly explained, "All right, now there are two different sources for where you can draw magic from. One requires you use magic from within. It is something like an inner strength, so to speak. The other source is when you learn it from books and teachings, which is what we are going to do now. Each time you cast a spell, it is the same as exerting your will to change your surroundings; therefore, it takes stamina to cast spells, and you might feel a little fatigue afterward. The greatest limit to anyone's magic is how much you think you can handle. Using a lot of spells is quite taxing to a person, but with enough determination and resolution, you can push past or even extend your limits of how much magic you can handle. Think of it being the same as exercising. The more you train, the more magic you can handle. That being said, for now you should take things slow with some simple spells. So, pay close attention to the movements described in the book, and I want you give the command to heal. In time, you can memorize the spell and will be able to do this without a command word. Just remember, something my teacher always taught me: 'The limits of your magic and the limits of your imagination are one and the same.'"

The symbol in the book was strange, but nevertheless, Revina still copied it, tracing it in the air above her hand with her finger.

Frank held his breath.

"Heal," she commanded, and to her surprise, her hand glowed

yellow and suddenly burst into flames.

Frank scrambled for some water as his new student flailed her hand around behind him, wailing; "Whaddo I do, whaddo I do?"

Frank took water from the flask and filled out a bucket from the camp. He held out the bucket, but Revina's flailing tripped him, and the water bucket soared through the air, landing on Revina's head, drenching her completely and at the same time, putting out the fire.

"Well, that went as well as I'd suppose for the first time. It would probably be better if you didn't use that spell in all honesty," said Frank. He looked at Revina's hand, which was now slightly burnt. "I guess we can do it the traditional way for now, follow me." After leading Revina to a greenish fern, Frank instructed her to crumple the plant, and rub it in her hand. "This is called Lady Fern; it helps with cuts, bruises, and can be used to help with labor pains in pregnant women, although you can ignore that last part. I'm pretty sure it's in that book on plant culture we got you." Frank then applied cold water and wrapped the hand in bandages.

"You know, the first spell I learned was Ignite. Maybe I should have started you off on that one."

"I don't think I want to set myself on fire anymore, thank you very much." Revina winced.

They still practiced the magic with fire anyway. And soon enough, after a couple of weeks in the woods, Revina was able to cast plenty more spells. She studied her books anew and trained to be fit enough to come close to out running Frank. Through his coaching, Revina was able to master the basics of magic, able to freeze water at just the touch, raise objects off the ground, and even summon a small ball of light.

"So, have you decided on which weapon you might want to master?" said Frank after looking at the pile of them laying in the corner of the camp.

Revina forgot about the weapons they had. "I don't know, what weapon should I pick?"

"Well, you could try them all; however, I think it would be best if you excelled using just one of them. Having multiple talents in each type of armament might only hinder you, because fighting with a shield and sword is very different than fighting with a bow. Just for now, try using whichever one feels the most comfortable to you."

Revina held the sword, shield, spear, and bow. None of it made any sense to her. She had no clue what stance she had to have or how to hold them.

"So which ones did you practice with?" she asked.

"None of them," Frank said matter-of-factly.

"But then what about that thing you carry on your back?"

"This," he said while drawing the metal staff, "is a mage's staff. Most of them are made out of wood and other flimsy material; mine just happens to be an exception. It's not something designed to fight hand to hand with, and they are very expensive, some of them go to be a thousand gold pieces."

Frank thought for a while, "Although I don't know how to teach you the specifics of how to wield each weapon, I can try teaching you the basics."

Revina shrugged and picked up the dagger, then they prepared to spar.

"Now, when wielding a knife, most often than not, your opponent will have a considerable advantage in distance, so try on working on closing the gap." Frank said as he kept Revina within an arm's length at all time, poking her in the head with his staff. He started gloating about it, while interrupting another of her attacks with another poke. "Finding it annoying, huh?"

Frustrated, Revina hurled the blade with surprising accuracy at Frank, who barely dodged it. The tree behind him was impaled with the knife, and after Frank removed it, he realized the hole was very deep.

"Not a bad idea to let your weapon close the distance for you, but never do this without some sort of back-up plan. Right then, as you threw the dagger, I had to take time to dodge, which you could've used to prepare a punch or kick—"

Revina interrupted him with a punch while he was talking.

Frank frowned and lightly massaged his cheek.

Revina smiled.

He poked her head again and gave her back the knife, "Okay let's try this again."

Revina began making sparring with Frank a daily habit and started to try out new methods and incorporate magic into the makeshift duels, trying blind Frank with that ball of light, or firing off bolts of fire at him to get him to come closer. Even though Revina felt like Frank was giving her a huge handicap by not using his own spells, she was still pushing herself to break past his guard. It was taking everything she had to avoid getting poked.

"That's it for now," Frank said after watching Revina sit down after another tiring day of training.

The only thing that stopped the training was eventually the lack of food left with what they bought from Yostel, not only that, but the amount of gold leftover from expenses was significantly less than one hundred coins. Frank looked over at the small pile of weapons left. The only one he'd taught Revina how to use was the one that made her the most vulnerable. And he couldn't teach her anything new about the others. What's more is he most likely taught her dangerous magic that she didn't understand the consequences of, further reinforcing his doubts as a good teacher.

"Well, it's high time we left and found some work. Maybe then we can find someone to teach you how to use the rest of these." He mentioned toward the weapon pile.

And with some time to get ready and pack, they finally left the Ether Woods.

Chapter Six
Finding a Master

"ICAN'T BELIEVE WE ENDED UP BACK HERE," SAID REVINA, looking at the beat-down furniture of the Worn-Down Mule.

"Yes, making a full circle was not exactly what I had in mind, but all the teachers in the villages around the Ether Woods would only teach knitting. I did tell you here in the city is where you could learn a trade, and that will be useful in the long run provided it's relevant." Frank dug around in his pouch for his last remaining coins.

"Also, this would probably be the best place in order to find some work." He turned to the bartender with the enormous mustache.

"You wouldn't happen to know where we might find some work available to some adventurers?"

"Depends if yer willin to pay extra."

"I haven't got extra."

"Well, bugger off then." The old man went back to polishing his glasses of beer. Frank just stood there, forming a very straight line with his mouth.

"That seriously can't be the way you ask for work," Revina scoffed.

"Oh, so you think, you can do better?" Frank retorted

"I *know* I can do it better." And with that, she walked over to the bartender, "Excuse me?"

"Yes?" The barkeeper was busy giving his drinking glasses a literal spit shine.

"Do you think you could tell me where I could find someone who needs help?" She asked him with a softer voice and beaming smile.

"Why sure, miss, there's a guild hall where they post flyers of potential jobs about two blocks over."

Revina went back to Frank, whose face hadn't changed.

"What is it now?" Revina asked

"It just occurred to me that we didn't bother looking outside on the street," Frank said.

Sure enough, there was a massive guild hall practically next to the Worn-Down Mule. With impressive arches and rising columns, it was rather hard to miss. Inside was a large gathering of all sorts of people, some looked to have very foreign clothes. Others wore full plated and rather expensive looking armor, alongside their opposites carrying old and cheap gear, such as the ones of two adventurers that just walked in.

"Was this place always here?" Frank wondered out loud.

After passing through the crowds of people talking among themselves, they came to a large wall with hundreds of flyers, with someone who was changing them and adding new flyers to the wall and taking down the ones that had a red "X" over them. When the man who was changing the flyers turned around; he surprised the two behind him, as it was the same old man as the bookkeeper and barkeeper, except this one's mustache had both of its ends braided at the bottom. Frank burst into a coughing fit.

"Say, you wouldn't happen to know someone who works in a tavern or library would you?" Revina asked the man before Frank could finish his coughing fit.

"Absolutely not," replied the quest keeper.

"This is getting creepy, how many of you are there?" asked Frank, but before the old man could answer, he reached out and grabbed one of the flyers that did not have a red "X" on them. "Is this one available?"

"Yes" said the quest keeper.

"Good enough, let's go." Frank left the before they could enter another long discussion with the man.

They left Yostel, and along the road, Revina decided to take a glance at the flyer for the job that they just took. It asked for the apprehension of a man on King's Road farther south of Yostel, but the man had no discernable features, just a footnote that explained he was located in the woods around the road.

"Are we actually supposed to be hunting someone?" Revina asked. "I don't know if I can handle that."

"Don't be silly, this should be a cakewalk. Look again at the flyer, do you see the reward money posted?"

Revina read the note again; it said the man was only worth five gold.

"You can use that as a way to measure the difficulty of the task," said Frank. "Since this is only five gold, it just might be some weird guy causing a ruckus in the woods. Starting off with an easy quest will be perfect for you. Finding him will probably be the hard part. My only plan so far is to go up and down the road until we meet him."

They were quick to find him. Frank was wondering how close they would have to get to the capital, until he suddenly received an arrow to the left foot, and instantly realized who was the man they were hunting.

"Son of a—"

Before he could utter another word, more arrows came from their right, off the road among the trees. Frank quickly took the shield from Revina and ran up the trees, blocking arrows from the attacker camping in the trees. The shield that Frank wielded could barely cope with the arrows that were being embedded in it, and as Frank threw the shield at the attacker, it shattered to splinters upon impact, knocking the archer to the ground where Frank jumped on top of him.

"Frank!" Revina shouted

"Frank?" questioned the archer.

Frank kept his weight on the man, "I'm over here. I'd like you to meet someone. This is Serge, the second-best archer in the Kingdom and the biggest jerk in all of Pravah. Serge this is uhhh . . . " he faltered

"Seriously? How do you not even know my name?"

"Well, you never told me."

"I'm Revina," she spoke to Serge instead of Frank now.

"Nice to meet you Revina, and what Frank just said is in fact false, for I am the best archer in the Kingdom," said Serge, still struggling under Frank.

"So, when I said you were the biggest jerk in Pravah, that was true?" added Frank

"No!" Serge finally pushed Frank off. Serge was a blond, also around the age of Frank and Revina. His demeanor and manner were fitting of that of a nobleman, but his patchwork clothes suggested otherwise.

"You two know each other?" Revina asked.

"Unfortunately, yes," Frank said.

"You know, it hasn't been much of a pleasure knowing you either Frank," retorted Serge.

"Can we focus on something more important? Frank still has an arrow in his foot. It can't be good to leave that in. We need to remove it and heal the wound." Revina was desperately trying to interrupt their banter and stop another fight from escalating.

"Don't worry about that." Frank lifted his cloak to show the arrow, which had penetrated his boot. But underneath the boot he was wearing iron sabaton and foot armor as well as greaves.

"Why are you wearing those?" Serge questioned

"It's because every bloody time we meet, it always ends up with an arrow to my foot."

"Not true, the third time in Angrost, I didn't even shoot you once."

"That's because I broke your bow before you could. And the entire time you were trying to stab me with your steak knife."

"Because you broke my bow! Do you know how expensive it was to get a new one? That meal you interrupted was the last I could have for a week. I had to skip lots of dinners to afford a new one."

Revina looked at the two exchange conversations back and forth. "You two are very good friends, right?"

"Absolutely not!" they shouted in unison.

Frank paused for a moment. "Wait, earlier you said you were the best archer. What happened to Grandmaster Johnson?"

"He died." Serge looked a little crestfallen. "He got old, it's as simple as that. At least he went peacefully about a month ago."

"He was Serge's teacher," Frank explained to Revina. "Does this mean you are the new grandmaster?"

"Well, maybe, I'm not very sure. I think I've heard some people call me that, but that was before I left everyone and didn't see any more people until . . .." Serge trailed off. "Yeah I haven't seen anyone until you two."

"So, you haven't seen another human being in a full month?" Revina asked

"Yeah, that's correct."

"Great, congratulations Grandmaster Serge, you now have a new student," Frank said as he pushed Revina into the newly appointed, panicking, and very flustered grandmaster.

"But I don't want a new student!" he complained.

"Well, now you have one, and if you do not teach her, I'll break your bow again." Frank eyed Serge. Serge could tell that even if he was joking, he'd do it anyway.

"On one condition. You do not get to interfere with the training in any way, shape, or form."

"Deal."

"Hold on!" Revina was not enthusiastic about being alone with the weirdo that spent a month being a 'nature man' with only himself in the woods. "Is this guy going to be my teacher?"

"Yes, and although he certainly doesn't look all that impressive—"

"Hey!" Serge interjected

"—he is still one of the best archers I know, and you can learn a lot by just spending some time with him. And I have a lot of respect for Johnson. Serge is his best student by far, that alone would be good enough for me to recommend him as a teacher. So, while you train with him, I will go turn in the quest, and if he tries to run away or shoot someone else in the foot, you can use him as target practice."

"Please don't." Serge was confused being praised and threatened at the same time.

"You're leaving?" Revina asked

"Yeah, I can't interfere with your training anyway. Besides, you'll do just fine without me." Frank was just about to leave before he turned around and reached into Revina's bag and brought out the book on hunting and trapping. "Just in case, using this might help."

Chapter Seven
All the King's Men

FOUR DAYS LATER, FRANK CAME BACK TO THE SPOT ON THE King's road where he found Serge, where a small campsite had formed. He couldn't believe how adapt Revina had become with the bow, and he was relieved that he put faith in Serge despite his many blunders. Frank watched as not only did Revina learn to hit the target from long distances, but she also used ignite and freezing spells on the arrow tips to make fire and frost arrows.

"That's all the basic training I can cover; the only thing left is to practice improving your accuracy and precision. That is something you can do over time, so make sure you take the time to practice. Sorry I couldn't teach you how to fire from horseback, but I don't have a horse, nor the means to afford one." Serge turned to the now emerging Frank, "Well? Where's the bounty rewards? I'm very hungry and taught archery for your friend, surely that means I get something, right?"

"Well, yeah, that's fair. But I doubt we can get that big of a meal for five gold . . ." Frank smirked

Serge's eye's widened. "Nooooooo, you can't be serious."

"Show him the bounty, Revina." There was an evil smile on Frank's lips.

Revina, confused, gave the flyer to Serge, who was outraged.

"FIVE MEASLEY COIN! I was the captain of archer guard that reported directly to the King! I was a leading substitute to the Elites! How dare- how DARE they!" Serge went ranting on like this for a couple of minutes, before finally yielding to Frank. "Fine, we can at least find someplace cheap to eat."

"About that . . ." Frank was no longer smirking. "I don't have the five coin. They won't accept the quest complete until I show them that we captured you."

"Well, of course, what did you think they would do? Just accept your word that you captured him somewhere?" Revina asked.

"No," but that was exactly what Frank thought.

"So, let me get this straight, while I spent a lot of time here teaching Revina, you're going to reward me by tying up my hands and feet, and drag me to Yostel like some freshly killed deer?" He glared intensely at Frank.

"Don't think of it that way, think of it more like you can clear your name with their authorities. And maybe," he drew nearer, whispering to Serge, "you can question them about that despicable price they put on your head."

Revina couldn't believe Serge would fall for such a lame stunt.

"I'll do it!" exclaimed Serge, completely falling for it.

"Off we go to Yostel, then!" said Frank, fueling Serge's enthusiasm.

Revina sighed at the stupidity of her two mentors, shouldered her pack, and followed. Along the path, some of Serge's ranting stuck with her.

She then asked Frank, "Who are the Elites? And what even is a grandmaster?"

Frank coughed. "Sometimes I forget how little you know. I guess I can't really explain who the Elites are without explaining grandmasters first. You see there are many different types of adventures out there. In Yostel's guild hall alone there were like thirty people. One thing that they all share is that they have weapons. And as such, those which are more skilled than others get recognized as masters. Each different class of weapons master is trained fanatically to the point where their weapon becomes a form of art."

"Currently, there are seven different types of weapon styles people like to use, archers being one of them. Duelists are those who train using a sword or an axe in each hand, making it difficult to defend against them. Assassins are trained in the use of knife and dagger, as well as a bunch of traps and lesser-known tools in order to surprise their enemy. Tanks use shields and tough armor to make a formidable defense. Swordsmen are taught how to keep a strong guard while at the same time breaking their opponent's. Spearmen use distance to harass their opponent, and mages do the same but with spells.

"With each class of fighter comes respective strengths and weaknesses, but the true importance of how to win a battle all depends on the individual. You see, grandmasters are those who push the limits of their weapon, and each are completely unique in a certain way. Call them trade secrets if you want, but that's what lets them keep their top spot despite the many challengers.

"A grandmaster is determined by whoever beats them in a one-on-one duel. Those usually take forever to verify as there are sometimes no one to witness it and can sometimes end in the death of the challenger or the grandmaster, but recently the numbers of those kind of cases have gone down. No one really knows how they originally came to power, because everyone's been selecting them this way ever since."

Frank paused, thinking of how to explain the next part to Revina, then continued, "The Elites were a group made up entirely of all the grandmasters; they were called together by the previous King of Pravah, Reginold the first. Before the group's founding, each class was feuding each other over which weapon was superior to the other, and grandmasters would fight amongst themselves.

Most times a grandmaster fought with another grandmaster, it ended with the death of either of them, or in even rarer cases, both. But when the Elites were founded, that altogether stopped. They reported directly to the King and worked tirelessly to keep the nation of Pravah at peace, inside and outside her borders."

Serge couldn't help but overhear, and some while after Frank's exposition, he pulled him aside. "Don't lie to her. Reginold was not the one who founded the Elites, and you know that."

"Officially, he was the one who created them. I'm just telling her what she would eventually find in the nation's history."

"I don't want my student to believe that rubbish."

"She's my student too, you know."

Revina couldn't hear any more of the hushed whispers behind her as they walked to Yostel.

They could not make it back before darkness fell, however, and they collectively decided to set a campfire to resume going back in the morning. For now, they had to feed themselves the few nuts and edible plants found in the foliage, much to Serge's disgust.

Soon, each of them turned in, but Revina couldn't sleep. She was staring at the wisps of smoke coming from the extinguished fire. How long has it been since the fires from Kupai? How long had it been since her father's blood was spilled? The screams of Kupai's townspeople still echoed in her ears. She was reminded of the way she lost her home, how she lost her family, and how she lost everything. Her throat welled up as she was about to cry, but her thoughts were cut short by Serge.

"When are you going to tell her?" he whispered.

"Tell her what?" Frank looked at Revina, who was doing her best to appear asleep.

"You know exactly what."

"There's no reason to tell her, and besides she's better off not knowing. The past is just that, the past. There isn't anything that can be said to change it, nor will it help anyone to dwell on it too much." Frank turned over, signifying the abrupt end of the conversation.

Revina couldn't help but feel like she was putting trust in some untrustworthy people. She went to sleep and had uneasy dreams. Those thoughts and feeling of uneasiness kept with her until morning when they returned to Yostel.

There, waiting at the gates, were the King's soldiers, lining the tops of the walls, and about a dozen of them armed at the entrance. Many were holding a drawing of a man that looked a lot like Frank.

"Sir!" One of the guardsmen stopped the party of three. "You have been identified by the citizens of Yostel to be a Mister Franklin Olsenhein and are found to be in direct violation of the banishment issued by the illustrious King Reginold the Second. This order was put into effect on the tenth of May, 4647, and you were personally notified during trial. How do you plea?"

They soon found that the other guardsmen had surrounded them, cut off their retreat, and had spears aimed directly at Frank. He couldn't help but notice the symbol on their shoulders was that of a blue dragon.

"I am not under the jurisdiction of the Kingdom of Pravah," Frank spoke very slowly. "This area of land is part of the provinces."

"Not anymore it isn't." The soldier pulled out a parchment adorned with seals and signatures from the royal capital. The most noteworthy of those signatures being King Reginold the Second himself! "Under the great law of King Reginold the Second, the glorious city of Yostel, her citizens and nearby lands are hereby annexed, and welcomed into the great nation of Pravah. Signed thirteenth of November, forty-six fifty-three."

"Now, the day of my sighting here . . . wouldn't happen to be November 12, would it?"

Revina looked back and forth at the spears being aimed at her. Those court orders being read off only came into power three days ago. What's more, the armor that the men were wearing also seemed very familiar.

The soldier did not answer Frank's question, instead brought out shackles, and immediately began binding Frank. Other men approached behind the leading soldier and took away Frank's staff and pack, Revina's weapons, and Serge's bow, breaking it in the process.

Serge let out a sigh.

The man who had just read off the two imperial decrees turned to Serge and Revina. "Are you two aware of the fact that you have been travelling with an incredibly dangerous criminal?"

"I just met him on the side of the road and followed him; we just happened to both be travelling to Yostel." Serge was technically telling the truth.

"I don't really know him that much." Revina followed Serge's example, and although she was doing her best to appear innocent, what she just said was painfully true.

"Well, either way, both of you will be taken in for further questioning. If what you've said is true, then you'll both be released by the end of the day." The solder signaled to the men at the top of the wall, which sent everyone scrambling.

From inside the city came scores of soldiers with the same armor, and the dozen or so men that had Frank surrounded were joined by fifty. From the closest woods to the city came even more men, hundreds all converged on Frank, who was bound in chains, and led him away from the city, marching in the direction of the capital. His staff was taken along with him. Of the hundreds of soldiers who left with Frank, only four remained with Serge and Revina. It all happened so quickly and normally that Revina almost forgot that there were hundreds of soldiers moving about. Why were so many people waiting here to arrest Frank?

"Right this way please." The four men led them through the opening square, which once had a bustle of people moving here and there, was now completely empty. All the men in uniform looked to have cleared out, and no one was up on the walls anymore. The party of six came to a court-like building that was ran by the town guard, none of which had a symbol of a blue dragon on their uniform.

"This way," the soldier repeated, somewhat annoyed. Two of the men separated Revina from Serge and led her into a vacant interrogation room, which held nothing but a wooden table with wooden chairs and cold stone floors and walls. She was then promptly left there waiting for what seemed like an eternity.

Chapter Eight
Seeking Answers

THE SILENCE OF THE EMPTY ROOM WAS BROKEN BY A MAN entering. He looked the same as the bookkeeper, barkeeper, and quest keeper from earlier, except this time the grey mustache was somewhat normal. It was just a semi-circle above his upper lip, making him look like a walrus, minus the tusks.

"Howdy," he said, "I'm the chief of the guard in Yostel. A couple of men from the capital told me that you were sorta seen with a nefarious criminal. Now I'm sorry I'm gonna have to be the big scary captain and ask ya some questions. So, how long have you known this man? His name was Frank, was it?"

"About a month ago, I met him in Kupai," she responded.

"Kupai? Wasn't that place . . ."

"Yes, it burned down. I lived there, and he saved me from the fire."

"You know, miss, we just have a report that the village was burned, but no testimonies from any witnesses. You and Frank are the only people that any authority knows of who were in Kupai before it being destroyed." The guard keeper scratched his 'stache. "If you know of anything about what happened there, it might help clear your name and the other guy's."

She retold the gruesome account of her father's death and the men in armor that burned down her village. She also told him about meeting Serge in the woods, eventually leading up to when they got arrested. After telling all she knew about Frank and Kupai, the man thanked her.

"Well, now, miss, you're free to go. I'm also very sorry for your loss. I'll make sure to write a report and tell the capital your account on the incidents in Kupai. The equipment that we confiscated should be at the front desk waiting for you," said the guard keeper.

"So, is it okay for me just to take my weapons back?" She was hesitant to why the man was letting her go so easily.

"Oh yeah, we get adventurers like you all the time, all sorts of disagreements like so and so didn't finish the quest the right way, or the employer lied about the reward, that kinda stuff. It's sorta unfair to withhold weapons from the adventurers that are just minding their business. Your case is a little more severe, but it should be fine to let you off. I have the testimony I need. Boy, it sure will be hard to find a way to deliver that paper all the way to the capital. We've sure been understaffed around here lately."

"If you're understaffed, why not try to ask all those men from the capital?"

"Well, there's only two of 'em. Plus, they sound like pretty busy gents."

"No, I meant the hundreds of guards at the wall."

"Hundred? No. There are only two capital guards in the city. Now, what could've gotten yer knickers in such a twist?" He looked at Revina's pale face, wondering if he did something to offend her. He breathed into his palm and smelled it; his breath seemed fine. He opened up a small mirror and checked his teeth. There didn't seem to be anything in them. He combed through his mustache, found a piece of chocolate, and ate it.

Revina, ignoring what the strange man was doing in front of her, asked, "So was no one stationed at the front of the gates earlier today?"

"Naw, those two fellas told us to clear out with some kind of legal mumbo jumbo they read off of a piece of paper."

"Wait, two? And not four?" Revina started to worry about Serge and where they could've taken him.

"Now why would there be four of 'em? Tell you what, I could sure use some magically duplicatin' guards to keep this city under order."

The old man got up to leave, but Revina beat him to it. She quickly got her gear to search the city for Serge. The whole situation reeked of suspicion.

⁓

Revina was doing her best to find Serge but could do little more than jump among the mess of crowds around the city. She needed a better way to find him. Climbing on rooftops, she found it easier to traverse the city thanks to the training she had in the Ether Woods. It took only a few minutes to find Serge in a deserted alleyway, along with the two missing capital men. Remembering what Frank said about hidden threats, she made sure to not be seen, and remained on the top of the building overlooking the alleyway. From her position, she could listen in on their conversation.

"You know, for this being official business, you guys are sure doing a good job of hiding it." Serge was responded to with a punch to the face. It didn't look like that punch was his first, as he was bruised badly and tied up against a wall.

"You've been doing an excellent job of staying in hiding, Mister Takker," the man spoke in a threatening tone. "All we want is information, and we'll let you go with a heavy purse for a new bow."

His partner grunted in agreement.

"I've already told you, I know just as much as the rest. I didn't really see him much." Serge received another punch. Revina noted that the first soldier was the one talking while the second just punched Serge.

"We know for a fact that is a lie. We have multiple records of you encountering Frank from city to city. You guys caused a ruckus, there's plenty of written complaints of a brawl in Angrost. Mister Takker, if you continue to lie, you will not leave this place alive."

His partner grunted in agreement.

"You're saying that like it wasn't going to happen anyway." He took another hit.

"Right now, your life is worth less than my lunch." The man held up a flyer for a wanted man with a five-gold piece reward. "So cooperate, and we'll let you continue your pitiful existence."

Serge fell silent and glared at the man. "Just for that, I'm killing you."

"Really? Tell me how you plan on taking me down? You're just some washed out archer who doesn't even have a bow!" Both of the men laughed.

Serge's restraints fell off, and he lurched forward, grabbing his interrogator and biting his arm before he could reach his sword. Revina chose this as a time to act and jumped from the roof on top of the other man. The interrogator's cry of pain was cut off by Serge clamping his hand over his mouth, and Revina held the other man at knifepoint.

"It's our turn to ask the questions now." Serge held the rope he just escaped with a mad gleam in his eye.

In a flash, the two who had captured Serge had switched places with him and were tied up against the side of the building in the alleyway.

"I'm going to have a few questions; first of which being who sent you? I want to know who your commander is, who tipped you off about our location, also why and where is Frank being taken?" Serge stood cross-armed in front of his new captives.

"And why should we say anything? You'll just kill us after we do," said the interrogator, mimicking Serge. The interrogator's partner added a similar grunt.

"Hey, Revina, could I borrow that bow for a sec? I'll give it back I promise." Serge took her bow and thanked her. He then immediately shot his aggressor in the foot.

The man doubled over and wailed in pain.

"Because I won't ask twice," Serge said with a menacing smile.

Chapter Nine
The Man in Chains

FRANK WALKED SILENTLY, SURROUNDED ON ALL SIDES BY hundreds of men. He noticed that they would frequently change guard with cavalry and positions in order to throw him off, but that was just fine; he had no plans on escaping. If he would run now, he'd just be persecuted until the next spotting of him in some village or town. Say what you will about the Pravah special guard, but they had an impressive intelligence network.

Frank then noticed that they finally reached the end of King's Road. The cohort of soldiers along with their one prisoner finally arrived at their destination, the capital city of Pravah, Angrost. It was impressively built, gleaming with iron plated walls and tall towers. It was sitting upon green farmland and was surrounded by nearby villages, which dotted the landscaped around it. This was the wealthiest city of them all, having many more businesses and buildings than in Yostel. Frequent trading caravans would enter its gates and leave with more goods.

The army leading Frank came to a stop at the gate, and almost all of them dispersed to the guard stations in the city, save for a group of twenty. At the very front of the procession, there was a man mounted on a horse giving the orders to the men. He was sharply dressed in plated armor that covered his face. His horse wore a dress called a caparison, and flags and banners adorned his weapon, a massive halberd. Frank was led right up to him.

"Follow." The knight signaled the men who he just sent up the walls to open the gates.

Frank was led through the streets of Angrost. Lots of onlookers pointed at the prisoner being paraded around by soldiers in uniform. Frank didn't like all the attention he got, but it didn't matter. What did matter was where he was going, the massive keep of the city loomed overhead. The group of people did not seem to be heading toward the dungeons of the keep, but rather going into its main entrance.

Through the doors of the keep was a large throne room. After entering, the twenty or so men fanned out behind Frank, covering all the exits and lining the walls. Now that he had a good look at them, they were more armored than the men that arrested Frank in Yostel, and had a blue dragon painted on the armor, almost exactly like the broken piece of armor in Frank's pocket.

"Welcome, welcome! Oh, great grandmaster mage!" the voice was patronizing and came from the throne. Reginold the Second sat there, with one of the armored men presenting Frank's staff to him like an auctioneer.

"Last time we met, your lordship, I wasn't so very welcome," Frank said.

"Ah, but that was in the past! I brought you here today to reinstate you as the court wizard." The King was being careful not to touch Frank's staff, only to inspect it.

"You made it very clear you wished to kill me, and not only that, but you also went after people who knew me closely. If you plan on having a repeat of the events six years ago, then I won't need my weapon to stop you." As Frank said this, chains that looked to be made of black smoke started materializing around him. The captain aimed his halberd at Frank's head, but the King held his hand up to stop him.

"There will be no fighting in these halls, nor do I wish to execute you yet. We all don't want to fight here, but if you push my hand, it *will* be like six years ago." The King put his hand on the sword in its scabbard. A red glow emitted from the sword underneath the scabbard, almost as if the blade was red hot.

Frank glared at the King, but his chains of smoke seemed to tighten around him, then vanish. The captain of the guard lowered his weapon, and the King took his hand off his blade.

"Why do you want me as the court wizard again?" Frank inquired.

"Because I only accept the very best to be at my side. If you are still the slayer of the Great Dark One, then you'll be fine. But just in case you've lost your touch, you'll be participating in this." Some of the armored guards brought over a large poster. On it read the title: "The Grand Wizarding Tournament."

"It's being held, right here, in Angrost!" The King rose out of his chair.

"Every mage and spellcaster from around the Kingdom, and some from neighboring countries, all are coming to participate in my tournament in which the grand prize is three thousand in gold and becoming the court mage to me. And there's another reason why this is being held. You see, the last grandmaster mage went into hiding for a very long time. As such it has left a lot of challengers waiting for a chance to prove themselves the strongest, so essentially . . ."

"Whoever wins this tournament of yours will be treated as the new grandmaster mage."

"Exactly."

"And if I don't participate?"

"You'll be executed, obviously."

Frank looked at all the soldiers around him. The King wasted no expense in preparing this; the armor they were wearing seemed to be enchanted for magic resistance. And every one of them looked to be well trained; it would be a pain to get past them bare handed. Not to mention the captain next to him, ready to slice him apart with the halberd.

"Fine, I agree to be part of your tournament."

"Splendid! Now, off you go! You are to wait in your chambers until the beginning of the matches."

And with that, the guards took him away. He was led up one of the tallest towers and was placed in a room where the sole window was barred, and there was no furniture, or anything in the room that could be fashioned into a weapon. Frank was shoved inside and could hear the key lock behind him after the door closed. He was only waiting for a few moments when a familiar voice could be heard shouting from outside the window.

"Oh, fair maiden! Locked away in the tallest tower! I've travelled the land far and wide for you to bless me with yon beauty! Please, I beseech thee, let down thy flowing locks, so I may receive a better look of thy fair beauty."

Frank looked down from the window to see his annoying travel companion, with Revina close by. "Knock it off, Serge."

"How are we going to get him out of there?" she wondered.

"Forget about doing that, try focusing on finding my staff and belongings." Frank didn't have anything important on him save for a gift from a friend. He'd hate to lose it.

"So, you just plan on staying in there?" Serge asked

"Well, I'm not staying long. Is there anything in town about some sort of mage tournament?"

"Yeah, there's posters all over the city about it."

"Good, come over and cheer me on."

"What?" Revina and Serge both looked at each other thinking Frank was being delusional.

"I said come cheer me on. I'm participating. Now leave before someone spots you."

Confused, the two left Frank.

As if tempting fate, the cell door behind Frank burst open. The captain of the soldiers who loomed in the doorway immediately started putting restraints on Frank and led him out of the room. Moving through the castle, they passed by many twists and turns. Eventually the narrow corridors gave way to a massive ballroom that was also cleared out of any furniture or items, just the same as Frank's cell.

This was when the knight switched his grip on his halberd, and Frank jumped back with good timing. The ground where he had just been walking now had a halberd cleaved in it. Seemed like the King wasn't waiting for the tournament in order to kill him. The great doors around the ballroom all at once closed, he could hear each one lock. There was nothing left in the room but the halberd-wielding knight and Frank, still in restraints. With a yell, the knight charged at Frank, who could just barely dodge and move around his attacker. He needed to escape, and he wouldn't be able to keep up with this man for much longer. The knight was immensely powerful. It looked like he could break through solid stone with those heavy swings. With each attack that hit the ground, Frank could feel vibrations. The cracked piece of stone floor where the captain ambushed him earlier gave him an idea.

After narrowly avoiding another massive swing from the halberd, Frank slid between his legs, then jumped, kicking him in the back. Angered, the knight gave another yell, striking at where Frank had landed, exactly the place where the floor was cracked. Frank rolled away and kept an eye on the stone tiles. They looked to be more damaged now. But that glance at the floor was a mistake, and in the split second that Frank lost focus, the knight made a jab with the tip of his halberd, connecting with Frank's left shoulder.

It wasn't enough to stop him. And now that the halberd was embedded in his shoulder, he had an opening. In less than a second, Frank grabbed the halberd using the restraints on his hands, leapt over the knight, and brought the halberd crashing down on the now immense crack in the floor. Frank's restraints broke open and so did the floor, sending both Frank and the knight tumbling below.

Chapter Ten
The Grand Tournament

REVINA HEARD A CRASH FROM SOMEWHERE IN THE CASTLE. "What was that?" she asked Serge, who was busy stuffing Frank's bag with some gold. Revina gave him a judging look.

"What? We're broke!"

Revina's face didn't change, Serge reluctantly put back the gold, and tried to keep talking in order to change the subject.

"That noise must've been Frank escaping. We should hurry up before the guards start inspecting this place." Serge and Revina were in the treasury room where all the valuables were being stored. It was also where that guard Serge interrogated said captured property might be held.

"You know, when I said hurry up, that usually means go faster." Serge was pacing behind the doors at the treasury entrance. He heard a large group of footsteps in the corridor and froze still, staring at the crack in between the doors. He saw soldiers hurry by, thankfully not aware that the guard detail at the treasury was inexplicably missing. He breathed a sigh of relief.

On his side of the doors, he poked an unconscious guard, who moaned softly.

"Still alive, very good. Revina! It's time to GO!"

"But I can't find Frank's staff anywhere!"

"If we stay here longer then no one will be able to find *us* anywhere!" Serge creaked open the doors a little to peek through. There was a courtyard outside the treasury, but everyone would be able to see them if they decided to cross. The entire palace was in chaos, with soldiers scrambling everywhere.

"What now?" said Revina, approaching the door.

Serge looked to the unconscious guards. "Strip them."

Using their new disguises, the two were able to get past the King's men surprisingly easy. This was mostly due to the fact that all of the guards were rushing toward the thunderous crashing coming from inside the castle. When they made it out of the courtyard, both assumed they were in the clear, until another one of the guardsmen behind them started running behind them in order to catch up to them.

Serge readied Revina's bow, but she stopped him. "Don't kill him. Think about it, what's the best way for Frank to escape? It will probably be the same thing we're doing right now," she whispered.

"There's like hundreds of guards in this castle, what makes you think it could be him?" Serge shot the man in the foot.

"SON OF A—"

"It's him," Serge verified

Frank waddled up to them, picking the arrow Serge shot him with out of his greaves, and taking the bow from Serge and shoving it to Revina.

"It's her bow, not yours!" Frank was out of breath, and the wound on his shoulder was hastily bandaged with a piece of torn cloth and seeping through.

"Are you all right?" Revina had never seen him this tired, not even when he fought those yetis.

"I am, just a guy giving me some trouble, that's all," he replied.

"One man?" Serge was in disbelief. Anyone who could actually wound Frank meant trouble. "Then we should leave Angrost, maybe go into hiding for at least a year."

"Did you recover what they took off me?" Frank asked, ignoring Serge.

"No, we couldn't find your staff." Revina said solemnly. She didn't know how they could afford enough money to buy a new one.

"That's fine, I didn't expect Reginold to leave it out of his sight. Do you have my cloak?"

Confused, Revina pulled it out of Frank's bag, "Yes . . ."

"Good," Frank breathed a sigh of relief. He helped himself to some better bandages and ointment for his open wound and gave back the rest of his pack to Revina. "Hold onto it for me, I'm going to go back."

"BACK?" Serge exclaimed. "Why would you want to go back?"

"Because that staff that they took is a one of a kind, and there can't be any replacement for it. I've got to go back for it. And another thing, they're not after you two; they're after me, meaning wherever I go, you two will be in jeopardy."

Serge paused. "Good point, let's go, Revina."

"Wait! Are you sure you'll be all right?" Revina looked at his wounds.

"I told you, I'm never sure. But I've got a tournament to get to, so you better be there to cheer me on."

Serge took Revina and went with his plan of going into hiding but did not leave Angrost.

Meanwhile at the castle, everyone was in uproar. King Reginold the Second was busy chewing out his commanding officer for letting the one prisoner he had under his custody escape.

"We agreed that we would wait to kill him! I knew I shouldn't have left you to your own devices. You should count yourself fortunate he only wrecked part of the building! Have you forgotten how he killed your friend? You would be dead by now if he used his magic at all!" Reginold was exasperated. "Did you at least check the surrounding area for him?"

"Yes sir," the knight responded. "No one has spotted a man that fit his description anywhere within the city's districts. We have also ordered a lockdown of the city, no one is allowed to leave until Frank is found."

"Wait . . . he couldn't be . . ." The King himself stormed up the stairs of the tall tower that held his most important prisoner and threw open the door. Sure enough, Frank was sitting there, covering up his now better-bandaged wound.

"Hey," he said.

"Don't you 'hey' me! You tried to escape!"

"I did no such thing. I've been in this room for the last couple hours. And speaking of the last couple of hours, there's been a major ruckus going on below me. Hopefully you aren't having any problems with any other prisoners."

Reginold was no fool; he knew Frank had a great chance to leave, so it must be because he was holding Frank's staff hostage. And since an attempt had been made on Frank's life, he would be more on guard. This would mean that he had to improve on the plan for the tournament, as well as increase the security for Frank's staff.

"Sure . . ." said Reginold, playing along. "I'm sorry I accused you. The tournament will be tomorrow, so I hope you have taken this time to prepare for it."

He closed the door on Frank, who just laid down and tried to get some rest for tomorrow.

⌒

The Grand Wizarding Tournament was every bit as grand as it was advertised. There was walking traffic from all the participants who had arrived from the gates, and the application and ticket lines to the events seemed to have no end. Everywhere, fans were waving the banners of their favorite mage, from the onlookers in the streets, to the windows from nearby houses. And a variety of booths were set up to sell food and souvenirs; it looked more like a grand carnival instead of a tournament.

Frank was wearing more restraints on him and being led to his first match by some of the armored men from the King's courtroom. He noticed that they didn't attempt to attack him this time. Instead, the soldiers just tossed him in a gated room off the side of a building, took off his restraints, and left him there.

Behind Frank, the gated doors opened revealing a huge stadium. It looked like a gladiator's pit with him standing at the bottom across from another mage. Loads of cheering fans were seated around the pit, many of them had purple banners, and it just so happened that the other mage had a purple uniform.

"Ladies and gentlemen, welcome to the first match of the Angrost Grand Tournament!"

Frank looked to see the familiar voice of the announcer, but immediately regretted his decision. Raised in the stands and in a booth sat the same old man from Yostel. This time, his mustache was huge, much bigger than his head, and the sides of it curled up.

"I will be your match keeper for today! And I'd also like to welcome his esteemed majesty, who has taken the time to be with us today!" The old man motioned to a decorated box seat, where Reginold waved from. The crowd erupted in cheers.

Frank looked throughout the stands for Serge and Revina, and he finally found them near the front of the crowd. Revina was waving and enjoying the excitement from the crowd. Serge was busy stuffing his face with some food from the vendors.

"Let's review the rules before the start of the match!" The announcer was projecting his voice with magic to speak above the crowd. "Even if this match is for who will become the future grandmaster, no killing of any kind will be allowed! The objectives are to knock out the other mage, or to stop him from being able to continue! You can use any spell you want *during* the match, but you aren't allowed to hurt the other guy before the fight begins! You are not allowed to place traps or poison your enemies beforehand! Now that that's out of the way, the bout will start when I ring this here bell, ready for combat!"

This tournament was strange to Frank. The King appeared to be making him go through a lot of unnecessary tasks, that much was obvious. Despite this, the best option would have to be to muddle through the challenges.

As the crowd's cheering died down, and everyone waited for the bell to sound, Frank found himself thinking about anything but this public spectacle. Ignoring his aching wounds along with the grumbling of his empty stomach, he wondered what he was doing back in this city he was never allowed to return too, and he thought about how he preferred it stayed that way. Still, he found himself dragged back to Angrost, why? He snapped out of his thoughts before the match started. Once the old man hit the bell, it took less than a second for the ground below Frank's feet to explode. His opponent's hands were glowing, and the ground where Frank just stood was replaced with a crater and a cloud of black smoke. Revina was horrified and was about to rush onto the pit, but Serge stopped her.

"Erm, that was a little unexpected," voiced the announcer. "Bartholomew has just killed Frank, and for that action, he gets disqualifi—" He was about to continue, but one of the soldiers in armor entered his booth and whispered something to him.

"Erm . . . I've been told that the rules have been changed slightly. If the death of a participant is accidental, then the challenger will not be held accountable. Furthermore, the challenger is also victorious." The announcer reluctantly decreed.

"So, then it would have been legal for him to kill me right there?"

The man in purple doubled back. Frank waved away the smoke

from the blast. He was untouched, even though he looked like he took the brunt of that explosion, he wasn't in the slightest bit harmed.

The purple mage snapped his fingers, and another detonation went off at Frank's feet. Frank emerged out of the following smoke-filled blast, still unscathed.

"I don't believe it! This mage named Frank is somehow negating all the damage sent off by Count Bartholomew." The announcer was standing on the edge of his booth.

The crowd cheered, and Revina was amazed to how little she knew about Frank, how was he being able to do all of this?

The wizard in purple took a dozen steps back, planted his feet, and snapped his fingers not just once, but about twenty times simultaneously. The crowd watched in awe as every square foot of the pit exploded all at once, save for an island of untouched ground where the purple mage stood. Smoke climbed high in the sky, and Frank was nowhere to be seen.

The purple mage peered through the darkened mist, and from it emerged a fist that sent him flying. Frank stood over his knocked-out foe, still unscathed from all of those explosions.

"I guess we have our winner!" The announcer shouted, and the crowd was mixed with cheers and boos at the unexpected outcome.

Frank was busy being led off the field by the men in armor. They rushed him away from all the onlookers who wanted to see the winner, and led him back to the cage he started the match in. To his surprise, he found Reginold waiting for him in there.

"A wizard is supposed to win with spells and incantations, not with his fists," he sneered.

"Well, I would've, but I didn't seem to have my staff on me."

"Listen here! If you don't abide by the rules, I will execute you!"

"Kind of hard to do if they keep changing all the time," Frank met his gaze. "I'd suggest you stop it."

"Stop what?"

"Stop trying to kill me. Why can't you let things be as they stand? You have an entire kingdom to run. Why are you wasting time with me?"

Instead of trying to play off his assassination attempt, Reginold eyed Frank and said, "Because, it wasn't too long ago when you were this kingdom's greatest threat. And till my dying breath, I will never forget the atrocities that you wrought!"

Reginold, annoyed, motioned for the guards to tie him back up then stormed out of the cell. He was going to go back up to his seat and watch the rest of the matches but was stopped by the purple mage who just lost the fight.

"I want to know what the hell just happened!" he said.

"Speak to me that way again, Bartholomew, and I'll have you arrested. You lost and that's all that happened." Reginold continued to move back to his chair but Bartholomew kept pestering him.

"I am a noble of the house of Quardo! I deserve to know what happened!"

"Your house means nothing here, nobleman! You stand in the Kingdom of Pravah! You promised me that you could kill any mage, but it's obvious you fell short of your own praising. To stop your intensive bickering, I'll tell you who he was. That man used to be the previous grandmaster mage."

"Then let me try again."

"Try again?! You couldn't even hurt him with several handicaps! You expect me to let you back in the tournament which you lost?"

"I know I can do it with another chance."

"What good would another chance give you?"

"A way to beat him!"

"Fine, either way, you are not getting paid anymore. This has been a huge setback."

"This isn't a matter of payment anymore, it's about pride."

Chapter Eleven
A Rematch

FRANK WAS BORED.
  Above his cell, there were all sorts of cheering and yelling about the tournament's arena, but he couldn't do anything but listen. The guardsmen had not fed him yet, which was bad. He lost some blood after fighting with that man with the halberd and needed some way to lick his wounds. There was no chance he would get some food though; Reginold would stop at nothing to kill him, even if it meant starving him in his cell. Next time he would get the chance, he'd ask Serge to bring him whatever he was scarfing down in the stadium.

It only took a few minutes and without asking, one of the armored guards came over and dropped him some food on a plate next to his cell, then left. Instead of eating the meal, Frank took the plate wiped the food off and onto the floor. If he could help it, Frank would rather not trust his captors. He then placed the plate back. Fortunately for Frank, the soldiers did not completely clean this cell like his previous one, and he was able to hide the food under some straw. After admiring a job well done of hiding the food, he sat back down.

Frank was bored again. The long stretches between matches were rather tiresome.

He waited for what seemed like hours listening to the cheering above his cell. It was interrupted however, when another guard jiggled his keys into the lock to open his cell. Behind him stood the very same mage in purple that Frank beat earlier.

"You!" The purple wizard was spitting as he talked. "You ridiculed me in front of a nation! You have tarnished my very name! And have cost me the hearts and minds of the people who were cheering me!"

"Ridiculed?" Frank sighed. "People lose in order for others to win. It happens all the time; no one really needs to ridicule you about just one loss."

"Well, they will now! You didn't just defeat me, you chose to humiliate me! Not even having the decency to face me in a magic battle! Instead of magic, you just used your fists like some brute!" He was getting angrier and louder.

"If you really are that upset about the standings, then you can always try next time," Frank calmly responded.

"The next time is now!" Bartholomew's hands started to glow. "I'll pay you back tenfold for the shame you've caused me!"

The guard who accompanied Bartholomew quickly ran back to get reinforcements.

"Shame?" Frank became restless and stood up straight. "You have not even an inkling of what *true* shame is! You still wear your colors, you have pride for being part of a group that chooses to give you standing, and you still choose to fight me. And above all else, you chose to blame others for your *own* shortcomings. YOU. HAVE. NO. SHAME."

Bartholomew glared back at Frank but lowered his hands. An armed group of soldiers came rushing back to help him, but he stopped them. Bartholomew, who came to fight, instead closed the door to Frank's cell and left.

෪

The next morning Frank awoke to captain of the guard visiting his cell. Frank kept an eye on his halberd as the captain opened the door. He strapped Frank into the restraints again.

"Follow," he ordered.

Frank was in rough shape. He hadn't eaten anything since he was camping with Serge and Revina before being arrested. And what's worse is that this guy was leading him to either another trap or his second match. Thankfully, the knight didn't do more than just take off the restraints and throw him into the arena, where Frank was greeted by blinding morning light and many cheers.

He searched through the audience for Serge and Revina and found them. He tried to motion to them for food by putting his hand to his mouth, but was interrupted by the announcer, who was the same old man with the huge mustache from earlier.

"Ladies and gentlemen, what we have here today is something quite unheard of, but it seems a match from yesterday was deemed a little unfair. There was an alleged reporting of some use of underhanded tricks. So, in the spirit of good competition, we'll have a do-over of the match from yesterday!" The announcer was met by murmurs and looks of confusion from the crowd.

"What they don't mention is that the loser was the one cheating," Frank muttered under his breath.

Standing across from him was the same purple mage from earlier.

Bartholomew's mind was racing, how was the man standing before him able to dodge all his spells previously? He couldn't see it before because of all the smoke that covered the arena from his explosions. Maybe if he tried using different magic, he might be able to find an opening.

He heard the announcer ring the bell and watched Frank very closely.

Frank took a step forward.

Bartholomew overreacted and snapped his fingers. A thick

cloud of smoke now covered Frank. He calmly took another step out of the smoky crater left behind after Bartholomew's explosion. The blast hid the way Frank was dodging the explosions, so Bartholomew couldn't tell what was happening.

He readied his hands again, instead of snapping his fingers, Bartholomew placed his hands on the ground. From it, spikes of ice rose toward Frank. Just as they seemed to reach him, they suddenly broke on impact, shattering, then melting, then evaporating into thin air. The crowd gasped.

"How did he do that?" said the announcer in disbelief. The crowd cheered.

From the stands, Revina watched as the purple mage threw spell after spell at Frank, who effortlessly deflected one after another. She remembered during training Frank telling her how spells might not work on him. But that didn't make any sense because she distinctly remembered that she used magic against him during the training too.

"Hey, Serge," she said.

"Yeah?"

"Why aren't any of those spells hitting Frank?"

"Come on, I thought I taught you to keep a better eye on things," Serge scoffed. "Look again at Frank just before a spell lands on him."

Revina looked carefully this time. Just before Bartholomew's fireball connected with him, chains that seemed to be made of smoke faintly flashed around Frank, and the fireball disappeared.

"What is *that*? Is that one of Frank's spells?" she questioned.

"How should I know? This is my first time seeing that." Serge furrowed his brow.

"Wait, but this doesn't make sense. I sparred with him earlier using magic!"

"Yeah, but did you actually hit him with any spells?"

"Erm, no . . . " Revina remembered constantly missing him,

but then again, whoever this mage in purple was didn't appear to be doing better than her at aiming spells, so then why was he getting hit? She carefully looked at Frank again, and he seemed tired, and the wound on his shoulder reopened and was slightly bleeding through his shirt.

"But why is he allowing himself to get hit?" she asked Serge. "Frank is suffering in that prison. Shouldn't we try to sneak in and try and find out how to help him?"

"Yes, I agree he looks a little worse for wear. If that guy who wounded Frank is still torturing him out in his cells, that could affect him in the long run. And if that's the same guy who's guarding Frank, then we'll be the ones in trouble if we attempt a rescue."

"Frank needs us! Are you a grandmaster or not?"

Serge was about to open his mouth in retort, then thought better of it. "Fine, I'll see what I can do after the fight. Until then, don't go off rescuing him on your own. The last thing Frank needs is you getting into trouble."

The crowd cheered, and in the gladiator arena, Bartholomew kept launching fireballs at Frank, thinking that might be his weakness. Frank stopped moving toward him; he seemed winded. Now it was only a matter of time until a spell knocked him out. At least, that was what Bartholomew thought.

Frank took a squat, slapping both hands on his knees like a wrestler. Bartholomew stopped casting spells, wondering what his opponent was doing with his peculiar behavior.

Frank was instantly on top of him in no time flat. He somehow managed to traverse a distance of six meters in one second, and while connecting Bartholomew's face with the length of his arm. Bartholomew was sprawled out, laying on his back, dazed after Frank's attack. He had a blurred outline of Frank looming over him. The first thing that came into focus was Frank's fist, rapidly approaching his face.

"No!" he screamed, just before being knocked out cold.

"There you have it folks. The winner is the new mage, Frank!" said the announcer.

Everyone in the stands was cheering, except for the King, sitting in his royal box seat. He motioned for his captain behind him to come closer.

"I want him dead," said Reginold.

"Yes sir," responded the knight.

"No, not Frank, the other one." He was pointing at the unconscious Bartholomew. "Can't have him blabbing our secrets, now can we?"

"You suspect he will, sir?"

"Maybe. He's quite unprofessional for a hitman. He had the audacity to ask me to arrange the prisoner's food poisoned and still couldn't win. And on top of that, he let his target escape him not only once, but twice. How *shameful*."

Chapter Twelve
The Great Escape

FRANK WAS BACK IN HIS CELL. HE HAD JUST FINISHED another match which went the same way as the fights with Bartholomew; his opponent used magic and was countered, and then Frank defeated them barehanded. And after his fight with Bartholomew, the King's attempts on his life appeared to have died down. Maybe he was running out of ideas on how to kill him. Frank could only hope. His thoughts were interrupted by the jiggling of keys in his cell door. Instead of the guard dropping the food on his cell like usual, he handed it to Frank personally. The guard pulled off his helmet to reveal Serge's grinning face.

"I don't know what's up with the security, but it's been pretty lax lately."

"Did you see any high-ranking guards, maybe one of them wielding a halberd?" Frank whispered.

"No, was that the guy who wounded you?"

"Yes." Frank was eagerly eating his meal, he spoke in mouthfuls. "If he's not keeping an eye on me, that means he's busy doing something of a higher importance. Now would be a good time to steal back my staff for me. You do know where it is, right?"

Serge had a guilty look on his face. "Umm, no, not really."

Frank stopped eating. "What have you been doing this entire

time then?"

"Well, I was busy finding you food! And not only that, but while I was out there . . . you know what they had?! A whole crapload of souvenirs lined up of all the contestants. You know, you're getting to be popular among the fans. So, they had some stuff of you, and just LOOK AT IT!" Serge pulled out one of the knickknacks from the stalls around the arenas. It was a wooden bobblehead of Frank.

Frank sighed and put his hand to his forehead. "So let me get this straight, instead of finding even the possible whereabouts of my staff, you decided to go gallivanting around the festival and buy toys? Where did you even get the money to pay for this stuff?"

"Umm, I may have sold . . . some of Revina's things. She wasn't using that spear and sword anyway, and I taught her incredibly well how to use that bow. Would've sold the knife too, but I guess she keeps that on her."

"Serge . . ."

"Yes?"

"Are you STILL upset that the King's men broke your bow?"

"YES, DAMNIT!" Serge confessed. "I tried borrowing her bow, but you wouldn't let me. So, in order to get the money for a new one, I sold what we weren't using." He turned around to reveal his new bow. "I bought it secondhand, so there's still some money left over, like maybe twenty gold."

"When we get back, the first thing you're doing is apologizing to Revina."

"Where is Revina anyway?"

"You're asking me?"

"Well, I assumed she tried to free you! I don't know where she ran off to."

Frank took a deep, very deep sigh. *This man is annoying.* Serge timidly approached him.

"Are you mad at me?" Serge asked.

"YES!" Frank snapped back. "I'll handle finding my staff personally, since you can't handle it. And just for screwing things up like you always do, give me the bobblehead."

"Aww, but I wanted to keep it," said Serge, reluctantly handing it over to Frank.

"You go find Revina, I'll finish the work on my end." Frank would've sounded much more impressive if he wasn't holding a toy version of himself.

∽

"You let him escape!" Back in the throne room, Reginold was infuriated with his captain. "I ordered that joke of a mage we hired to be killed, or did I not make myself clear?"

"No sir, you were clear," the knight quietly responded.

"Now you're telling me he found some way to leave Angrost? You know what that means, right? He's just going to find some way to go back to his stupid house of Quardo, and I would need to have a war with the entire nation of Frant!" The King sighed and sat down in his throne. "This tournament is starting to become a disaster. How did you even lose track of him in the first place? He was unconscious in the arena when I told you to kill him!"

"Well, sir, in order to spare your good name in the eyes of the people, I followed him until he ventured into Angrost's most popular bar, the Spittoon. He had a couple of drinks, then set up a teleportation circle. He must've done it beforehand as he was able to activate it quickly, most likely hiding it somewhere in the bar."

"Have the circle destroyed immediately, and the Spittoon owner fined. Do we know where the circle's destination is?"

"There's no way to know for sure, but my suspicions guess he's somewhere in Frant."

"Well, then, find him! You are now responsible for clearing up the mess with this Count Bartholomew!"

"But sir . . ."

"I know how much killing Frank means to you, but you've messed it up too many times. So, I shall personally see to Frank's death myself! You are now placed in charge of the execution of Count Bartholomew, and if you screw this one up, the next to be executed will be you!"

Reginold's knight stiffly bowed and then left to carry his duties. He was replaced by two of the armored guards behind him. They happened to be the same two guards who interrogated Serge.

"Sir, there's a problem with the prisoner," said the interrogator.

His partner grunted in agreement.

"Then take me to his cell right now!" replied Reginold.

The interrogator shrugged and led the King to the jail. The group of three made their way down to the dungeons of the arena. When they made their way to Frank's prison cell, it was empty, save for one bobblehead figurine in the center of the cage.

"You know, technically we still have him under custody," said the interrogator.

His partner grunted in agreement.

Reginold looked at the toy that resembled Frank. He then slowly turned his head to his two guards. "You brought me all this way, just to tell me he escaped?" he said menacingly.

"Uhh, maybe?" the interrogator said sheepishly. "We didn't think you would believe us if we just told you. That . . . and you just ordered us to take you to his cell."

His partner grunted in agreement.

Reginold massaged his forehead and took a very deep sigh. "I want you two to report to securing Frank's staff immediately, no doubt he's probably going to target that next. If you two decide to screw that up, I'll send you to patrol the frozen proveniences for the next twenty years, got that?"

"Yes sir," said the interrogator. His partner grunted and saluted. Then, the both of them scurried off to secure Frank's staff.

～

Serge finally found Revina. She was hanging off the side of the castle keep's walls, peering into one of the windows. Serge approached the base of the wall she was on, which was about twenty meters under her.

"Hey!" he called out to her.

Revina looked down to see Serge waving back up at her. Using rope, she slid down to him, rappelling off the side of the castle wall.

"I found where they're keeping Frank's staff!" she said.

"That's great, now I- I mean we, can tell him where it is!" Serge was thinking that Frank would forgive him for his mischief. "Where did you find that rope anyway?"

"Oh, I bought it using the money you got for selling my weapons." She jingled a bag of coins at Serge.

He checked his pockets and couldn't find his twenty gold. "Uh, you knew about that?"

"Yes, I do."

"Sorry."

"It's fine, I needed to sell them. All that extra weight was heavy. But from now on, either Frank or I will hold onto the money since you keep spending money on those vendors around the town's square. For now, can you climb up there and find a way to steal his staff back? There's a lot of guards and I don't know what to do."

Serge climbed up Revina's rope and checked the window she just looked through. He didn't see any guards in the room, and the altar in the center of the room was empty.

"Where's Frank's staff?" Serge shouted to Revina.

"It's right there! Surrounded by all the guards!"

"The room's empty."

"What?"

"The room's empty!"

"Impossible, I just checked it like a minute ago."

"What are you two doing?" The question came from behind Revina made her jump. It was Frank, and on his back, he carried his staff.

"Umm, we were just about to get that for you." She pointed at his staff.

Serge descended with the rope, falling on his face just before reaching the ground. "So, we have all we need, yes? Good. Now we can leave this place behind us and run to someplace where the King's men can't reach us. Maybe one of the provinces he hasn't annexed yet, or a neighboring country." He was talking as if Frank taking back his staff alone seemed natural.

"No, I have a better idea," said Frank. "I still have one more match that I have to do in the tournament, the finals. Sadly, all the mages I've faced this far have been lacking. I'd be damned if I let one of these simpletons become the new grandmaster."

"Wait, you actually want to become the court mage?" asked Serge.

"No way."

But then you'll just get trapped again by all these guards," argued Serge.

"Not unless every citizen in the Kingdom knows that I am the grandmaster."

Serge scoffed, "You're crazy, there's hundreds of guards in this city and they're not just going to let you do whatever you feel like, grandmaster or no."

"I have to go back, Serge. If I don't, then Reginold will stop at nothing to hunt us down, and I don't want to leave this issue unfinished. How can I call myself a grandmaster if I don't show up to my challengers?"

༄

"Umm, sir?" The interrogator and his mute partner faced a very angry and growingly impatient king.

"Didn't I just tell you, less than five minutes ago, to guard Frank's staff?" said Reginold with an acid tongue.

"The problem with that . . . you see, is that the staff was already stolen by the time we got there, and all the guards that were assigned earlier are unconscious." He could see the King growing angrier with each word he spoke.

"Surely, since this didn't happen under our watch, and . . . because of your infinite kindness . . . you'll spare us the punishment of sending us to the frozen wastelands?" said the interrogator fretfully, with his eyes avoiding to make contact with the King's.

His partner grunted in agreement. Nodding his head furiously up and down.

Reginold clucked his tongue in annoyance. "Do every single one of you idiots have boiled cabbages for brains?!" His shouting echoed through the courtroom.

He then sighed and slumped back down in his throne. "Since it was as you say, and the theft happened after you were assigned, I'll give you one last chance to save yourselves from banishment. I want you both to search for Frank's staff while I get ready to announce the winner of the grand tournament."

"Yes sir, a most gracious offer, sir. We are not worthy of such mercy, sir." They both shuffled away, repeatedly bowing their heads as they did so. Then, they exited through the Keep's doors.

"Right, they are about being unworthy," Reginold muttered to himself. "Should've killed Frank when I had the chance. Maybe he really did have the better approach, and I only got in the way." Reginold regretted being cruel to his second in command.

Reginold's out-loud thinking was interrupted by the Keep's doors opening again. The interrogator and his partner ventured back inside before the King.

"Didn't I just tell you, less than five minutes ago, to find Frank's staff?" Reginold sounded even more menacingly.

"Well, we found it. It's in the arena."

"And why, pray tell, haven't you brought it to me?" The King's tone was becoming downright venomous.

"Well, err, because Frank has it."

Reginold rubbed his temples. His entire guard was massively incompetent.

The plan of the tournament wasn't to allow Frank to be anywhere close to the finals, and now he was in them, meaning he would no doubt win them. It was customary for the King to give prizes to the winners of the tournament, being the host and all, but he couldn't see himself giving Frank the win with a straight face.

"Here's what you two are to do. Gather every single guard in the city and go to the arena and wait for my order."

The gloves were off; there was no way he would let Frank win.

Chapter Thirteen
The Grandmaster Mage

FRANK WAS HAVING SECOND THOUGHTS ABOUT SHOWING UP. Everyone in the arena was at a standstill. Since the King had to be present during the final event in the tournament, everyone was waiting on him. Frank couldn't help feeling like he was hurting his chances of escape over the time they were wasting standing around.

"There he is, ladies and gentlemen!" The announcer was the same old man with a mustache that was too large for his head. "The King has just arrived!"

Everyone clapped for the King, who was finding a seat in a raised box.

"Now without further ado, I shall announce the participants of the Grand Tournament finals!" The crowd cheered in response.

"On the side to my left we have the mage in a tattered white cloak, Frank! He has shown to have a gift for avoiding spells and has kept his magic a secret up till now!" There were more cheers for the announcer and for Frank.

Frank focused on his adversary. He had asked for Revina to give him back his cloak and staff for the finals because he was planning on leaving before getting captured again. He was busy investigating his opponent, who was also in a cloak. Whereas Frank's was white and ragged, his opponents was ashy grey and in slightly singed at the edges.

"On my right we have Cinis, a newcomer who specializes in fire magic! Both mages have been undefeated in this tournament that has held magicians and sorcerers from across the world! Whoever wins this match has the right to call themselves . . . grandmaster!" The announcer was met with more cheers from the audience.

When the cheering finally died down, the mustached announcer hit the bell.

Nothing happened. Where others were quick and eager to hit Frank with spells, this man, Cinis, watched Frank just as well as Frank watched him. There was an uneasy silence, or there would have been, if Serge wasn't having a coughing fit from the stands after his food went down the wrong way. Revina embarrassingly patted his back.

Serge's coughing distracted Frank, and the moment he looked away, Cinis fired a huge cone of flame. Fire filled the arena, but it parted around Frank like a rock in a stream. Unlike the spells from the other mages, Frank deflected the flames made by Cinis still circled around the arena. Cinis fired more fire spells, which in turn circled around Frank, making him grow uncomfortably hot. Cinis kept up the pressure, firing more fireballs at Frank; the magic wasn't affecting him at all, but the heat was intense.

"Wow, folks! Cinis looks to be holding Frank on edge with his fire magic!" said the announcer.

It was true; Frank had no opening. His opponent knew what he was doing and surrounded Frank with walls of flames. Those flames were getting closer and were slowly cooking him alive, but rather too slowly. Cinis was appearing to be giving Frank a chance of surrendering. That must mean he wasn't after Frank's life like Bartholomew.

Frank thought to himself that there would be no shame in losing to a mage like this. The man before him spent almost as much time researching magic as himself. Frank could just give up. There was no need to pick up the burden of becoming the grandmaster mage again. And maybe if he went back into hiding, Reginold would leave him well alone.

But through a break in the raging fires, he saw Revina's worried face among the stands. He couldn't give up just yet; that girl still needed help, and she reminded him of someone he once knew. Those memories took him back to a grave on a hill full of white flowers with a lonely oak tree resting on top.

His cloak caught fire. That snapped him out of it.

Giving a loud yell, and summoning immense will, he slammed his staff into the ground, like a blacksmith's hammer on an anvil. The resulting shockwave knocked everyone out of their chairs and sent Cinis tumbling. The rushing air put out most of the fires.

Cinis got up quickly but was met with a sweep to the legs with Frank's staff. Thinking fast, Cinis propelled himself backwards with fire, anything to put distance between himself and Frank. The tide had turned, and Frank didn't want to give an opportunity for his opponent to escape. He threw his staff as if it were a javelin, with its tip bouncing off of Cinis's shoulder. And while the staff was still in midair, Frank grabbed the other end and brought it crashing down on Cinis, rendering him unconscious.

The announcer was speechless. He and the crowd behind him stared with their mouths gaping open at the massive crack in the center of the arena where Frank hit the ground.

The King stood up in his box seat above the announcer and pointed directly at Frank. "Seize him!"

The King's command brought hundreds of soldiers filling the stadium. The clanking of metal was loud and brief. The soldiers surrounded Frank and pointed their spears at him, their captain was not among them.

"This man is a danger to our country and our people!" The King's shouting silenced the confusion from the spectators. "He is the very same mage who I have banished from this kingdom six years ago! For the crimes of killing the previous Grandmaster swordswoman, Eleanor!"

"Don't you DARE speak her name!" Frank was angrier than Revina had ever seen him. Around him the chains made of thick black smoke materialized, before she could only see glimpses of them, but now they were noticeably clear.

"See! Look people, he wields the magic of the Great Dark One!" The King's words sent everyone in the stands into a panic. The announcer was nowhere to be seen, and the spectators were climbing over their seats for the chance to leave the place.

Serge looked at the mass confusion of the crowds. They would not have another chance to leave. "We gotta move, now!" he said urgently to Revina.

"Now where are you two off in such a hurry to?"

The following grunt confirmed Serge's fear. Their paths were blocked by the interrogator of the guards and his accomplice.

The arena, which had held an overabundance of fans, was now empty, save for Frank standing above his fallen opponent, surrounded by troops, with his two friends being held hostage. And above him sat King Reginold the Second, holding all the cards.

Chapter Fourteen
Confrontation

EVERYONE WAS ON EDGE. WHAT SHOULD HAVE BEEN THE finale to a merry tournament was now turning into a deadly showdown. In the center of the stadium, all of the guards were aiming their spears and swords at Frank, making sure to cover all the exits. The chains of black smoke around Frank were coiling around him, much like a snake. His fury and anger were clearly shown, and he was giving the King, who was standing a building's length above him, the deadliest glare.

"We've found his accomplices sir!" The interrogator shouted from the stands. Serge and Revina were also surrounded, but by considerably less men than Frank.

"Accomplices? Someone's actually trying to help him?" Reginold was baffled. "Are you even aware of who the man you're trying to help really is? He's a killer!" He pointed at Frank. "That man has more blood on his hands than the entire city combined! He is a threat to peaceful existence and cannot be allowed to run rampant!"

"Your hands aren't so clean yourself." Frank's tone fit his angry scowl. But he could not meet Revina's gaze. She was looking about hopelessly, not knowing who to believe.

"You are responsible for the death of grandmasters! You are

responsible for the death of the previous king! Those are irrefutable!" yelled Reginold.

The King faced toward Serge and Revina. "I have been granted this position of power from my late father, and as such he entrusted the safety of this nation to me. As a king, I have come to a decision, for death to come swiftly and harshly to Frank. Those of you who allied with him must either help slay this evil man or be branded criminals! Know this: that every second you help him, you are helping bring the end of the rest of our lives!"

During his accusation, Frank remained silent, not uttering a single word and continuing not to make eye contact with Revina or Serge. Serge took this time to speak up.

"Frank, I have only known you since for the last five years. Even then you were extremely reclusive. I do not know why you felt the need to lie to me or to Revina of what you've done. We are cornered and threatened with death. If you do not tell us what happened when you were leader of the Elites, then . . ." Serge aimed his bow at Frank's head instead of his foot.

Revina couldn't believe her ears. Frank was a grandmaster mage? Serge wasn't holding back any more secrets, but it was barely enough to explain anything.

Serge's mind was also racing. Grandmaster Johnson would always praise Frank as a young genius. Had he been fooled the entire time thinking Frank was trustworthy? Had Frank changed over the years being a grandmaster? Serge couldn't keep his aim steady on Frank; he only had that problem once before. Back when Johnson took him hunting for the first time. They were chasing a wild boar, and when the animal was cornered, it would give little regard for its own life, and lash out at its aggressors in front of it. That's what Serge was aiming at now, a cornered animal.

"Revina, you need to escape. This is no place for you to be," said Serge.

"Agreed, let the woman go, and make sure there are no

spectators caught in this. Get Cinis to safety." Reginold was realizing there was only one way this would end.

Two of the soldiers slowly approached Frank and dragged the still unconscious Cinis out of the arena. Frank didn't move.

"No! Frank, why won't you tell them they're lying? Why won't you say anything? You were the one who saved me in Kupai! Surely that doesn't you an evil man . . ." Revina looked at him with tears in her eyes.

Frank finally met her gaze. "Leave, Revina," he simply said.

She felt betrayed, going through all of this effort to trust him, and he doesn't even want her here? "I'm not leaving!"

Frank took half of a step forward, Serge let loose his arrow. Frank deflected it with a spin of his staff. All of the soldiers charged him. As soon as that happened, Frank counterattacked. It was as if he grew a sixth sense. He began to duck and roll through the soldiers' attacks and parry each and every single swing at him. He knocked them out with blows to the head, one at a time, jumping from soldier to soldier. And was slowly making his way toward the stands.

Serge was doing his best to hold back Revina, who was yelling "Stop it!" at the top of her lungs. The interrogator and his partner left the two in order to reinforce the King.

The center of the arena turned into a pit of chaos. Frank used the uneven footing of the cracked earth from his attack on Cinis to his advantage. Dodging to and fro, he leapt over his opponents, dispatching them from left and right. He spun his staff around so quickly, changing his grips on it almost seamlessly, connecting with the skulls of his aggressors, dispatching them one at a time. He would jump over their swings and hit them with a punishing overhead axe kick, and when dodged under their swings, he'd finish with an uppercut from his staff. But there were hundreds of soldiers, and they were beginning to overwhelm Frank. The chains of black smoke around him were repeatedly tightening on him; his staff lit up but could only manage a flicker before extinguishing.

One of the soldiers stabbed Frank's back shoulder. Frank grabbed the soldier and threw him away, and another one stabbed him in the leg. Frank was barely hanging on, hitting his aggressors away, only to leave an opening for them to inflict another wound. Frank was slowly dying and bleeding everywhere. He could not afford to lose; he made a promise not to die.

"No!" Revina was still being held back by Serge, who she was desperately trying to push off.

"ENOUGH!" Frank's voice thundered, the chains of black smoke around him shattered. The staff Frank wielded was crackling with so much immense power that he overloaded his shadowy bindings. The supreme willpower he conjured made his staff shine with a blinding bright light.

The soldiers covered their eyes, and that brief moment gave Frank some time. He rose his staff upwards, and from the sky, a massive meteor the size of a castle came hurling toward the arena. Everyone scrambled for the exits. Serge took away Revina, kicking and screaming. The King and his bodyguards were already gone, and some of the soldiers retreated.

The ground shook, knocking over some soldiers, amidst the confusion the light on Frank's staff faded, and the chains of smoke rematerialized, wrapping around him. Frank looked like he was struggling against his own magic, and it was the last thing Revina saw before she and Serge dove for cover.

The meteor completely destroyed the entire stadium. Rubble flew everywhere, damaging the nearby buildings and devastating the soldiers. Fireballs split off the comet and were raining down on the city, causing destruction and mayhem. The mages from the tournament, Cinis among them, were casting shields to protect the residents of Angrost. Most of the city was saved, but not the mess of rubble that remained of the tournament's arena.

Chapter Fifteen
A Promise Kept

THE KING'S SOLDIERS PICKED THROUGH THE DEBRIS following the aftermath of Frank's attack, finding any of the wounded and escorting them away. The end to the Mage's Grand Tournament left an area of devastation in the city of Angrost. The soldiers freed two more survivors from the ruins; they were Serge and Revina.

"Those two are civilians. Get them to a relief shelter." It was the interrogator who coordinating the relief efforts to the men cleaning up. "Treat them well; they helped us to try and stop all this." He held out his hands to the damaged city.

His partner gave orders to the soldiers as well, but only in grunts, so the men were confused. The interrogator would follow up behind him and reissue the orders. The men gently carried Revina and Serge up to the castle alongside many other injured soldiers. They split off from the groups of wounded men and left them in one of the chambers alone. Eventually, a physician came in to check on them, concluded there were no extreme injuries, then left.

Revina was silent and looked away from Serge.

"Even if we wanted to, we couldn't take on all those guards; this is the only way we could be allowed to stay alive," he said.

"Frank isn't alive," she muttered.

"There wasn't anything we could do for him."

Revina looked away from Serge again. She spent all this time training, all this time preparing for when one day she could help someone in need. And when the day came where she had the chance to help the man who had once helped her, she did nothing. Now, Frank was dead, just like her father, and like all the people from Kupai. She buried her head in her knees and refused to look up.

Serge kept silent. There was little that he could do to console her.

Days passed, the guardsmen brought food, but Revina didn't touch any. Her grief was interrupted by the captain of the guards who came in to question them.

"My name is Quil, head of the guards here in Angrost and second in command to Reginold."

Serge looked at the weapon on the man's back. Surely enough, it was a halberd. He must've been the one who wounded Frank.

"I've come here to ask the two of you about the whereabouts of Frank, the dangerous mage who blew up the Mage's Tournament colosseum," said Quil.

"Frank's whereabouts? But . . . he's dead," Serge said.

"We have reason to suspect that he has escaped. His corpse was not found anywhere in the rubble, and his staff was also not recovered," explained Quil.

Revina looked up. There was hope Frank was still alive?

Serge was skeptical. "He was caught in the middle of the explosion, perhaps he and his staff were completely destroyed."

"Maybe the body, but not that staff. We believe it's made of Lonsdaleite, material that's tougher than even diamond. It won't be so easily destroyed. If it's missing from the tournament, that means Frank still has it, and he escaped somewhere." Quil was still upset that he couldn't see to Frank's death personally, and wanted to make sure, in every way possible, that he was deceased. "Since there are many reports of your valor against Frank, I want the both of you to search the city. If you come across him, or anyone in the city who could've met him, I want you to report it immediately to me. Find a guard, and they should be able to direct you to me. Otherwise, you are free to go"

Quil then escorted Serge and Revina out of the castle and left them in the city. Revina still looked depressed to Serge. He suggested to actually start seeking Frank, if only to keep themselves busy.

They tried searching Angrost for any signs of Frank to no avail. Everyone was still picking the pieces after the attack, so no one could give any information on a mage in a tattered white cloak. Eventually, Serge and Revina split up to find Frank, Revina settling in on a bar named The Spittoon to ask questions.

It was packed, there were plenty of customers, and the furniture and stools were much better than the ones from the Worn-Down Mule.

"What're ya havin', miss?" Sure enough, the bartender was the same old man as the bartender from Yostel. This time, he had mutton chops instead of a mustache.

Revina ordered the cheapest beer.

"Why so gloomy? Is something wrong miss?" asked the barkeeper.

"I lost someone," she rasped out, trying to keep her voice steady. "Do you know of any wizard in a white cloak?"

"No, can't help you there. Was he lost in that big explosion?" Revina nodded.

"Truly a terrible thing. Did you hear who was responsible for that incident? The guards said it was the loser of the Grand Tournament finals!"

"What?" Revina was confused. "Cinis didn't cause that explosion . . ."

"You daft? I said the loser, not the winner. Apparently, that mage, Frank, lost the bout, got all angry, and blew up the place. Not a very sporting fella, ain't he? I hope he gets what's coming to him."

"NO!" Revina's worried shout made everyone in the bar go silent. Looking awkwardly around she said, "We should try to focus on rebuilding the city and treating the people who were hurt by this."

The onlookers from around the bar nodded and returned to their conversations.

The barkeeper drew close to Revina and whispered; "Look, I know you're a little confused. I am too. I was *there* watching that match when Frank beat Cinis. But we can't really talk about it; after everyone evacuated the stadium, the King's men issued this decree on a really long parchment that Cinis was the new winner."

"Wait, you were there? Could you be related to the announcer?"

"Absolutely not. Although I hear he is quite handsome." The barkeeper scratched his mutton chops. "Anyway, that's not the point, you're really lookin for Frank, ain'tcha?" he whispered.

"No, I'm just looking for a . . . friend."

"Well, either way, there's usually a reclusive person of sorts, he comes by every now and then, but his last visit was years ago. A feller in a cloak like you said, usually visits the cemetery, plants a flower, then leaves." The barkeeper went back to polishing his beer glasses and pretending like the conversation they had never happened.

Revina understood the gesture, paid, and then left the Spittoon.

⌒

Revina couldn't find Serge in the city before going to the graveyard, so she decided to go on alone. Angrost's cemetery was located outside the city walls, along a path leading to the base of a small hill. The graveyard itself didn't have that many dead and was deserted of any visitors. It was what was on the hill that caught

Revina's eye. A large oak tree was at the very top of the grassy mound, surrounded by thousands of white petunias, which made the entire hill dazzle with the white flowers.

At the very top of the hill, next to the oak tree, stood Frank in front of one more grave that was separate from the rest. He was soaked in his own blood, and barely standing, but managed to lay down some flowers on the grave; more white petunias.

"I'm sorry, Ellie," he murmured. "I couldn't keep my promise." And he then collapsed in front of the tombstone.

Revina swiftly ran up behind him to catch him; he was unconscious. Frank was badly hurt and needed medical help. Revina readied a healing spell, but even while unconscious, Frank's chains of black smoke sprung up and nullified her healing spell. She used whatever bandages she had on her and carried him on her shoulders to look for help.

In Angrost, it was hard to stay hidden with a dying man on her back. The weight on her shoulders made it so that all she could do was wobble forward. Frank smelled metallic as he left a trail of blood behind Revina wherever she went. She was about to turn another corner into an alleyway to avoid the guards, who were on high alert, when she bumped into Serge.

She looked at him with fear; he might turn Frank in to Quil. But instead of outing her, Serge took a look at Frank, who was still bleeding and unconscious.

"Come with me. It's not safe here. We need to stop the bleeding and get him to Yostel. I know someone there who could help him," Serge said.

Revina looked at him with grateful tears in her eyes, "Serge. Thank you."

"I know, I know, cool it with the waterworks. We need to focus on saving this fool here." Serge said humbly.

Serge left Revina, and then quickly came back with a rented carriage to take them to Yostel, no questions asked. Before Revina could ask how he could afford this, she noticed the bow he'd left with was no longer on his back. Guess he really was a good friend.

Chapter Sixteen
Reunited

I T TOOK MORE FINESSE TO GET FRANK THROUGH THE STREETS of Yostel, but there was less of a guard duty than Angrost, and they were able to make it in front of a house in the city. Serge knocked on the door.

"Let me do the talking," he said.

A woman opened the door and was shocked at the number of people. Serge opened his mouth as if to say something but was denied the chance by a slap to the face.

"You vanish for weeks, don't even bother to visit, or write me letters, and now you show up here with a guy who's already half dead, some girl, and where's your bow, huh? Did you break it again?" With each word the lady spoke, she was pummeling Serge.

Serge opened his mouth to say something but was silenced by another slap to the face.

"What have you been doing? You don't just ditch me and leave me here with no one but myself!" She was still giving Serge a smack with every syllable.

Serge tried again to say something but was stopped by another slap.

"Erm, excuse me? Serge said you might be able to help him." Revina motioned to Frank on her back. "Please help us, we don't have anywhere else to go to save him."

Serge gave Revina a look of gratitude for interrupting his beating. The woman now noticed the gravely wounded Frank, and her demeanor quickly changed to a more professional attitude.

"Sure, quickly bring him inside." The woman opened the door wide and went inside, clearing out a table. "Set him down right here." She gave Serge one more slap to the back of his head, before going into another room.

She came back quickly after changing her clothes into a nurse's uniform and putting on gloves.

"Is there anything I can do to help?" Revina asked.

"Yes, go to the market and pick up alcohol ointment. It should be on left of this street." The lady dropped some coins in Revina's hand.

Revina quickly got the ointment and then came back. She made an effort to avoid the stares she was attracting in the market from the bloodstains on her back. "Anything else?" she asked the woman treating Frank.

"Yes, make sure that idiot doesn't go anywhere." The nurse pointed a bloody finger at Serge, who was doing his best to appear innocent.

"I would never—" he started.

"Save it!" she hissed.

"Yes, dear," he mumbled.

It took hours, but Frank's breathing steadied, all of his wounds cleaned, rinsed, and stitched, and he was expertly bandaged. Revina thanked the lady through her tears. Frank was still alive. The nurse took off her gloves and put a blanket over Frank.

"He lost a lot of blood; it will take time for him to recover." She left to the next room to wash her gloves and change.

"You're a miracle worker, 'Belle!" Serge said.

"Don't you suck up to me now!" she shouted from the other room, although it was clear the nurse liked it. She came back, wearing the same clothes she had when greeting them. "I've stitched his wounds and disinfected them. Lucky for him, all of his organs are fine."

"Thank you, Thank you so much." Revina was gratified to this person, but realized she knew her almost as well as Frank, which is to say, very little. "What exactly was your name again?" Revina asked.

"It's Isabelle."

"Thank you, Isabelle. My name is Revina, it's very nice to meet you."

"Likewise. Who is the man I just saved?"

"Franklin Olsenhein. He used to be praised as the greatest mage of all of history. He was the one who found the Society of the Elite Seven, known as the Elites, in secret and gave credit of the accomplishment to King Reginold the First. And he is the one who led our nation, also in secret, against the Dark Crisis. An event that occurred during the Pravian Civil War six years ago," Serge interjected.

"Dark Crisis? Serge what are you talking about?" asked Revina.

"That's just it, I *don't* know. I spent years as captain of the archer guard at Angrost. I went through back channels and everyone I could bother in that castle, and I got little to nothing. Apparently, there was some huge operation to destroy any history of it existing. All I do know is the Dark Crisis involved some creature called the Great Dark One who threatened all of Pravah, and after the Elites faced it, the group disbanded. The only one who knows more about it is the King, and this oaf right here." Serge flicked Frank's foot. He still remained unconscious.

"The Pravian Civil War?" Revina gravely spoke. "My father and I fled to the frozen provinces to escape that war."

"Once he wakes up, we'll force him to explain everything, or I'll shoot him in the foot, wounded or no." Serge annoyingly muttered some stuff to himself, then left to buy food and to find any more news from Angrost in Yostel.

Revina was alone with Isabelle.

"So, how did you get to meet Serge?" Isabelle asked.

Revina held up the bounty she got from the quest keeper, "Frank and I were trying to do this."

Isabelle burst out laughing, "FIVE GOLD? HA! Can I keep that? I want to have it framed on my walls above the fireplace mantle. I'm sure he'll hate it."

Revina acquiesced and gave her the bounty. "How do *you* know Serge?"

"Oh, he's my boyfriend."

"WHAT? Serge has a girlfriend?"

"Yeah, I know what you're thinking; he is kind of a weirdo. But he's very sweet when he needs to be and dependable like no other. My father was the late grandmaster archer Johnson, rest his soul. I met Serge when he became my father's student. He was exceptional . . . good-looking . . . and he fancied me." Isabelle framed the bounty and put in above the fireplace, just below a silver-colored bow.

"That's a family heirloom," Isabelle said, noticing Revina looking at it. "My dad, on his deathbed, wanted Serge to become the new grandmaster. But the only way you could become a grandmaster was by defeating the original, and my father, in his weakened state, couldn't possibly fight. So, Serge refused and instead did his best to comfort Johnson before his . . . death." She sniffled a little.

"Word got out, somewhere along the way, that the famous Grandmaster Johnson was dying, and his position was up for grabs. That nasty rumor brought hundreds of foolish archers that wanted their arrows to be the ones that ended my father's life. They believed that because he would die anyway, why not let him die for their own gain. It was sick and twisted logic that was only a front for their greed."

Revina could only listen to Isabelle's story, but she wasn't the only one listening.

"They couldn't land so much as a scratch on my father, however. That was because Serge decided to duel them, every single last one of them, so that they couldn't hurt Dad. He spent sleepless nights accepting so many challengers, sometimes still with arrows in him from the previous matches, but he still won. Every brawl, every challenge, every fight, until my father finally went. His last words to me were, 'give him this and protect him as he protected me.'" Isabelle cried holding her father's bow.

"After Serge learned that he died, he didn't lay one finger on the bow and disappeared. I haven't even heard from him till now. How was I supposed to protect him when the entire time he's in hiding?" Isabelle sniffled.

"Aw, Belle!" Serge opened the door also with tears in his eyes; he'd been listening. "My greatest mistake was that I made you cry; won't you ever forgive me?"

"No," she sniffed. "You don't get off the hook that easy, and you were eavesdropping." She put back the bow.

"Please?" Serge hugged her tight and kissed her deeply.

"Well . . . maybe a little . . ." Isabelle said.

Revina was red in the face sitting in front of the two lovers. She cleared her throat. Embarrassed as well, Serge and Isabelle quit kissing.

"Aww, don't stop on our accounts," Frank said.

"Wha-d-d when did you wake up? How long were you listening to our conversation?" Serge sputtered.

"Around the same time you put your ear to the door, which is to say, all of it. You know, for an archer, you have very loud footsteps." Frank calmly responded. "Don't stop now, you were just about to make out with your girlfriend."

"The moment's ruined!"

"Okay fine, I'll leave then."

"NOT SO FAST!" Serge pointed a finger at Frank. "You have

a lot of explaining to do. And not just to me, you got to tell all of us."

"Tell you what?"

"Everything! Start with the very beginning. My entire life was just put on show, so it's only fair that you do the same, Frank. We've risked our lives to save you, not to mention maybe becoming criminals for helping you. There's not one written page about your history anywhere in the Kingdom, so you need to tell us." Serge stared intently at Frank.

"There's been enough sob stories today. I don't want to bother everyone with mine." Frank tried to get up to leave, but winced in pain, then laid back down on the table.

"Cool it, hotshot. You're not fit to move anywhere, and you need your rest. You're staying on that table until you get better," Isabelle ordered.

"Okay, thank you for treating me." He turned to Revina. "Was it you who brought me here? The last thing I remember is visiting a grave in Angrost. Where am I now?"

Revina nodded. "We're back in Yostel. I found you at the grave, and I tried to heal you, but I couldn't."

"You shouldn't heal people with magic, Revina. It's not reliable." Frank was stern. "I knew I was a bad teacher; I should've explained that more clearly. If you were able to perform the spell on me, I might have—" Frank stopped himself short, he was lecturing the girl for saving his life. Admonishing her recklessness while he was doing the same this time was just hypocritical. "Sorry, I got ahead of myself a little. What happened next?"

"Then Serge even helped me save you and sold off his bow so we could travel to Yostel. The two of us met Isabelle here where she treated you," Revina continued. Then, after some silence, she opened her mouth again. "We want to know what happened back at the Grand Tournament."

"All of you are better off not knowing," he said.

"Please, Frank." She looked at him with big eyes. "We need to know what happened to you. You're our friend."

Frank took a long exhale, trying to figure out where to begin.

"Some time ago, there was a coup within Pravah, and a great monster was unleashed on this kingdom, which I had to defeat. After a long battle, where I was the victor, the monster cursed me to never use magic again."

"You can't . . . use magic? But that spell at the tournament . . ." Revina wondered.

"The curse is a spell in and of itself. Ergo, I can still use magic, if the spell I cast is stronger than the Great Dark One," Frank explained.

"But, why did the King call you a murderer? What happened to you in your past?" Revina asked.

Frank looked down in shame. "Because I am one," he said softly.

The room went silent.

"Frank, give us the full story," said Serge with arms crossed. "What happened to you?"

Frank let out a very long sigh. "Fine," he submitted. "What I'm about to tell you has a reason for being so secret."

Chapter Seventeen
A New Tale

MY NAME IS FRANKLIN OLSENHEIN, WHAT'S BEEN SAID OF me is quite true, very painfully true. My life has been rather depressing, but it isn't to say I didn't enjoy it. I have had plenty of bittersweet memories, along with the regrets of the mistakes I once made. Maybe that's just me being jealous of how I used to live. There might always be some part of nostalgia that makes me think somehow the past was better.

I led a rather spoiled life as a child. I was born into a noble family, so that let me obtain an excellent education compared to most. My father and mother, being noblemen of Pravah, had a say in the politics of the nation's court, and often gave advise to the King, Reginold the First. Isaac, my father, was a favorite of the King, and my mother, Lisandra, would manage many of his meetings. They were an influential tag team who were able to gain plenty of admiration in court.

Even if they were very busy, they gave me all the love and support I could ever ask for growing up. As their only child, they adorned me with gifts and lessons. My early life was essentially happy. However, good times just don't seem to last, because as my mother and father grew in popularity in the court, so did the jealously and greed of the other noblemen.

Two of them, Count Montegew and Duke Jeffrey, became the ringleaders of an operation to undermine both of my parents. One day, we came back home to find our house robbed, looted, with many structures broken beyond repair. There was no search to find anyone responsible for it, and some of the guards were bribed with nobleman money to fake a report of the crime. They constantly stole anything of value from my family, and the Duke and Count would refuse many appeals made by my parents to see the King. They virtually took over the court from both of my parents. King Reginold himself held little interest in courtly matters, as he declared himself to be a warrior king. I believe maybe he suspected that it was normal for power to change in court, and so my parents' pleas fell upon deaf ears.

Still, we somehow managed to get by. After becoming the poorest noble family in our nation's history, we sold off any belongings we had left in order to keep up appearances in the palace. My father only had one fancy dress attire to wear at ballrooms which had constant holes, and because of his appearance he was branded the unfortunate nickname of the Pauper. My mother kept up with her activities, but now they were in secret, and she would never attend her own gatherings. Both of them, tired as they may be, still kept up with my education no matter the consequence.

The frustration I had growing up became too much to bear. Looking at their worn out faces everyday sprung even an eight-year-old to decide that something is wrong. Perhaps it was childlike heroism, but I decided right then and there, that I would do everything I could, no matter what it took, to ease my parents' burden. I turned to practicing magic. That's where my own adventure began.

Chapter Eighteen
The Hermit

A T AN EARLY AGE, I WAS EXTREMELY PASSIONATE AT LEARNING magic. My aim was to find a position as the court mage to eventually help my parents, and if there was a solution, it could always be found with study. In a short four years, I went through every instructor in the capital. I exhausted all my teachers until they ran out of material to teach. When that happened, I would simply move to another teacher until I ran out of teachers. I soon became known as a prodigy in the city of Angrost. Eventually, there was only one mage left to learn from, the grandmaster mage before me, Old Man Magoo.

He was holed up in a shack some distance away from Angrost. Seldomly accepting visitors, and shying away from society, he was as reclusive a hermit as they come. People made sure to steer clear of him for good reasons, as there were all sorts of rumors about him. Word was that out of the hundreds of applicants he had, only two other students were admitted, both of whom died while under his training.

So, naturally, being young and stupid, I threw all caution to the wind and visited the hermit to learn more about magic.

The very instant I knocked on his shack door, I was met with a professional curtesy befitting that of the greatest wizard of the time.

Out of a hole in the wooden doorway, an eyeball peered through.

"Whatdoyouwant? Goaway! Ihavenointrestinyou." After saying this in approximately one second, the eyehole was plugged up with a cork.

I knocked again.

From inside the shack came a muffled voice, "Go away!" along with some strange purple light. The welcome mat below my feet, which read "Not Welcome," began to raise. It carried me off his land, into a nearby ditch, and dumped me there.

Frustrated, I marched back up to his door and knocked again, this time not standing on the welcome mat. The not-welcome mat then curled around me like a tongue and flicked me away from the shack and back into the ditch. I marched back up to his house, only to be defeated by the mat again. This was repeated several times.

I spent a full day fighting that rug. When nighttime fell, I stood above my fallen quarry. The sheds of the broken fabric and carpet burns all over my legs and arms signified my victory. I knocked the door again.

"Go away!" said the voice again, along with more purple light.

Nothing happened. I knocked the door again.

"Willyoustopwiththatinsistentknocking?!" The cork was removed and replaced with an incredibly angry eyeball. Magoo was giving me a one-eyed glare, then saw me standing over his destroyed creation.

"No! Not Matthew!" The eyeball looked sad, then went back to glaring at me. "C'mere you!"

After this, the door swung open, and a long spindly hand dragged me inside along with the remains of Matthew.

༄

Old Man Magoo was just as his nickname hinted – he was old. With a constant hunched position, and a closet full of bathrobes, he looked like some pitiful Merlin. Although, pity is not a good word to describe him, because he was powerful, smart, and exceptionally strict. At first meeting me, the kid that spent a good part of the day pounding away at his door, it was fair to say he didn't like me. Despite being bothered by me, he still had enough patience to take the time to learn about me.

"Whoareyou? Whattdoyouwant?" said Magoo. He was pointing his wand at me and kept me spinning in midair, essentially interrogating me.

"I want . . . to learn more about . . . magic," I said, still spinning. All the revolutions were starting to make me queasy.

"No. I don't teach anymore. Now go home." Magoo spun me away into a pile of books. He went to stitching his not-welcome mat back together. After finishing it, he poured some blue potion on it, traced his finger on the carpet, and gave a command: "Vita!"

The rug sprung back to life, hugged his arm, and then slid back underneath the door.

Amazed, I just stood there with my mouth gaping open. "How did you do that?"

"Magic. Isn't it obvious?"

"Then why won't you teach me?"

"I'm not allowed to teach anymore. Surely, you've heard about me? I hurt some kids, and they said I was too strict. Hmph! Silly mages . . ." Magoo drew closer with a nefarious glint in his eye. "*Why* do you want to learn huh?"

"So-that I-I can help my parents," I stammered.

"Help? You want to learn magic to help? My how naive you are boy! You want to help people become a doctor, become an architect, or choose some other profession."

"But I want to learn!"

"Then learn something else. You want to know what magic is really used for?"

I nodded.

"Magic is power, raw power. We humans will always be

irresponsible with that. Magic is used to harm, to subjugate, to *kill*. That's what it will mean to become my student." Magoo turned his back toward me.

"You know, it is true . . . those rumors, I know you've heard of them. Practically anyone who knows of me, they know of those rumors as well. I hurt my students before. They didn't respect magic, just the same as you. You should leave, go back to your happy life, and leave me well enough alone." Magoo went back to his experiments.

I still didn't leave. I kept pestering that old man, every morning till the evening of every day I would fight Matthew and come into his shack to watch his experiments. At first, he refused to teach me. I would only watch him perform his magic, going through his steps on my own afterwards. He had all sorts of amazing spells, arrays of potions and rare ingredients holed up in that shack, as well as a small library of dozens of books on magic. I would constantly sneak into his possessions, doing my own experiments and screwing things up in the process. I happened to constantly be causing a mess in his laboratory.

Old Man Magoo eventually had enough of me. After giving me several beatings, he set magic traps outside his shack to aid in Matthew's defense. They successfully stopped me, but only temporarily. I would continue to come back, constantly testing out the traps and finding ways around them. The traps grew increasingly crazier. I remembered at one point he grew a giant Venus flytrap bigger than the shack itself to ward me off, but I still managed to get through.

"FINE!" Magoo exasperated on the morning I got through his daily traps. He glared at the small boy who somehow was found to be sitting on top of a giant, dead, Venus flytrap. "FinefinefinefinefineFINE! I'll teach you magic! You wanna blow things up, you wanna freeze things, you wanna become an arsonist, FINE! As long as you leave me the hell alone!"

In the following years, I was put through the most rigorous training imaginable. I had to promise my parents that I would return soon. There was no holding back, and after Magoo accepted me as the student to the grandmaster mage, Magoo magically packed up his shack in a small bottle and pocketed it. We then set out to tour the world.

Chapter Nineteen
Trial by Fire

MAGOO WAS THE WORST TRAVEL COMPANION YOU COULD think of. Every question I made about our destination would never get answered.

"Where are we going?" I often asked.

"A place."

"Where?"

"That isn't here."

It was as if I was talking to a brick wall with him. It seemed as if our travels really did lead to anywhere that wasn't "here." Our travels didn't just stop at exploring all of Pravah and the nation's surrounding provinces but went on to neighboring nations such as Frant. Most of the journey was not spent in cities; however, as the first stretch of the adventure, we travelled south of Angrost, into the Rotten Forest.

It was safe to say the Rotten Forest was in fact, rotten. There wasn't a trace of green anywhere in them. The ground was a deep shade of purple, and the waters looked polluted. The twisted trees and misty landscape gave a chilling atmosphere that spoke you do not want to enter this place. Which is exactly where Magoo and I were heading into.

"Are you sure if we're going the right way?" I asked.

"Listen here, boy, if you want to get anything done, you're gonna have step outside of your comfort zone every now and then. So, start being unsure of things, start to question things, and find the answers to such questions. You can't spend all your days holed up with mommy and daddy."

Oh, he sure did take me out of my comfort zone. He made me be the one leading the path in the Rotten Forest and did little to no helping at all. I was supposed to chart a course through a territory I've never been through before, so of course I ended up getting us lost.

"I don't think I've met someone with a sense of direction quite as bad as yours," Magoo critiqued.

I am fairly sure I had some sort of pained expression on my face when I was with him in those woods.

It didn't take a long time for monsters of the forest to see the two lost adventurers as easy prey. What was strange about the Rotten Forest was that the things that emerged were not just some animal or bandit, but instead the trees themselves! The decaying trees around us steadily *removed* themselves from the soil and began lumbering towards us. Magoo sat down cross legged, refusing to help me even in the slightest, as I ran away from trees chasing me.

"Come on, boy, you can't run away from all those trees forever! They'll eventually corner you, then whatcha gonna do?" he taunted me. Why the trees seemed to be ignoring him was beyond me.

"Alliges duplicia!" I shouted.

Vines sprouted from the ground and wrapped themselves around the decaying trees. The trees simply unrooted themselves again.

"Now why on earth did you think that would work?" Magoo criticized.

Panicking now, I dodged and ducked their branches.

"Come on kid! Overcome your odds using your magic! Remember that the limits of your magic and the limits of your imagination are one and the same." Magoo's advice was oddly inspirational, but it didn't help me with the trees.

Eventually, they did overwhelm me, just as Magoo predicted. Cornered, I readied my hand to perform another spell.

"Flamma!" I yelled.

The trees caught fire, being old and dry, the fire spread quickly to all of them. This completely stopped them in their tracks, there was no more danger. I was proud of my work, but Magoo wasn't. He took me by the ear and hit me on my head.

"Whatdoyouthinkyou'redoing? You dope! You fool! Using fire magic in forest full of old trees! Look at what you've done!" Magoo pointed around us.

Sure enough, the fire spread way too far, trapping the both of us. The moving trees ran into the woodlands off the path starting more fires off to the distance. Magoo readied his wand and stretched it into the sky, it glowed bright, and a crack of thunder was heard overhead. Light rainfall begun slowly putting out all the fires I caused.

"Thank goodness, I don't think we angered the spider." He said.

"You can control the weather?!" I exclaimed.

"That's cataclysmic magic. Please tell me you know what cataclysmic magic is."

I shrugged.

"Seriously? What did your previous teachers do with you? Babysit?" He sighed.

"You see boy, in magic there are three rungs; Basic magic which alters whatever's around you is the lowest rung. The next tier of magic is cataclysmic, which changes things over a city or a nation. The last level is apocalyptic magic, that which changes things on a global scale. They say no one has used that kind of magic since . . ." Magoo's expression darkened.

"Since when?"

"Since magic itself was created." Magoo picked up his things and continued on the path through the Rotten Forest. He refused to speak any more about the subject.

That didn't stop me from peppering him with questions. Ranging from when and where magic came from, to what exactly is apocalyptic magic. For some reason, he pretended not to hear me when I talked about apocalyptic magic, so instead I choose to ask different questions.

"Why did none of those trees attack you? I was right next to you when it happened," I inquired.

"Peh! Probably because you're so darn weak. Isn't it normal when animals hunt to go after the easy prey?"

I looked at the hunched over old man. A stiff wind looked like it could knock him over. I wasn't buying it.

Trying to change the subject from how weak I was, I asked more questions. "Earlier, you mentioned a spider?"

"Oh yeah, that damnable beast. Technically, we may be somewhat close to her hunting grounds. But even you couldn't get us *that* lost." Magoo looked at me like he doubted if that was really true.

I crossed my arms, annoyed, and stopped asking questions.

We continued being attacked by more monsters from the Forest. All sorts of beasts and creations emerged from the woods, and Magoo would send me headfirst into any danger we encountered. I was set upon by snarling wolves, abducted by giant birds and forced to fight them in midair, and faced off against massive golems. There seemed to be no end to the Rotten Forest, but we somehow made it through with little to no help from Magoo.

Chapter Twenty
A Gruesome Lesson

A S WE LEFT THE ROTTEN FOREST, WE CROSSED OVER Pravah's borders with her southern neighbor, Syracoosa. Magoo barked at me something along the lines of this is where we would be setting up the "camp" and tossed at me the bottle which held his house, expecting me to place it down. Nervous, I somehow uncorked the bottle and popped out the house back to full size without any accidents. I think I heard Magoo grumble something about beginner's luck.

"All rightythenyougoshdarngreenmuffin!" he started.

Did he just call me a muffin? I thought to myself.

"We're now beginning the training, young'in. I'll be having you constantly casting magic till you puke out yer innards. The only rest you're allowed is for sleep and food, the only breaks you're allowed will be on dangerous treks through the furthest reaches of this known land!"

"Huh? We're just now starting? I thought we began in the forest . . ."

"That was just a leisurely stroll."

"A leisurely stroll?" I asked, pained.

"Yes," he smirked. His superior attitude annoyed me somewhat. We went through his entire library from his shack. Every spell from every book numbered somewhere in maybe the hundreds of thousands, and he forced me to memorize as much as I could, which isn't to say very much. The rest that I couldn't memorize I had to write down in my notes. He forced me into applying what I'd learned through sparring, and the combat with him was rough. He always used the spells that I would forget how to counter or avoid. It's almost like he could tell exactly what I was struggling on and mercilessly exploited them every combat I had with him. In short, he would pummel the crap out of me whenever I slipped up.

Breathless, after another of his sparring, a thought crossed my mind.

"Why don't you ever teach me any magic that isn't for combat?"

"Eh?" the noise he made resembled a goat somewhat.

"Well, you've making me practice fire magic, ice magic, how to harness lightning, the ways to move soil and cause earthquakes, the creation of objects, illusion magic and how to cast light, how to influence plant life, even the ways to create small hurricanes and storms," I said, making sure to count each subject on my fingers so that I wouldn't forget.

"So? What of it?" he said.

"Why haven't I learned healing spells? Or other magic that might be useful to others?"

Magoo grew angry. That wasn't to say he was usually cross with me, but at that moment, his disapproval at me was much more apparent. His eyes furrowed, and his hunched-over stature loomed over me.

"I told you what we are boy, or have you forgotten? Magic is a *weapon*, not something to help others. Those 'priests' as they so call themselves who try to use magic to heal people are fools. Leave medicine to the doctors who are much more qualified than you and me to save a life."

Magoo then did something even stranger. He grabbed me by

the arm and took me into the forest. The entire time his grip on me never loosened, and he didn't utter a single word. He led me around that forest by the arm for hours on end till he finally found what he searched for. We stopped in front a small clearing. In the center of the clearing, there was a deer that must've been attacked by some sort of wild animal from the dangerous woods and escaped. It was bleeding out from bite wounds on its stomach, and it didn't look like it was going to make it.

"There's always victims near the edges of these woods." Magoo finally let go of me. "Go on then," he gave me a grim nod. "Perform the spell."

I stood in front of the dying deer. It was too weak to get away. Magoo stood next to me, unflinching.

"I-it's not a spell I practiced . . ." I began.

"You looked it up in secret, no? You are a prodigy, after all. I doubt you don't know how to do it." He did not look at me; his eyes never wandered away from the deer.

I was terrified. Beads of sweat trickled down my head. My throat was dry. Magoo's attitude was far from normal, and it was putting me at edge. He was right of course I had looked up the spell without him. I did my best to calmly approach the deer, although I was anything but calm. To make me attempt a healing spell I've never attempted before was making me more anxious than anything.

I held my hand over its wound, my hand started glowing green, and I said, "Tempus fugit!"

The deer, which had been weakened considerably, let out the most awful bleat. And I watched in horror as the wound I tried to heal began to rot and decay from the inside out. The creature which was peaceful not even a minute ago was writhing and twisting, all the while screaming in sheer agony.

I was in panic and tried to back away from the animal.

"Don't you DARE look away." Magoo's threat made me stop in

my tracks.

The deer's shrieking became more garbled as the rot travelled from the wound to its throat as well as the rest of its body, eventually its noise ceased altogether. Its legs, which were busy flailing around maddeningly, now twisted, contorted, and fell off the deer's body, with the muscle fibers of the animal not able to support the weight of its own bones. The deer's face went hollow, and its cheeks sullen. The eyes of the animal melted, and the gelatinous ooze of what used to be its eyeballs streamed down as if it were tears. After some agonizing time finally passed, the only things left of the creature was its skeleton, laying on top of a large puddle of greyish-red mess.

My hands . . . they would not stop shaking. What I did was beyond torture. It was sickening.

"I-I can't b-believe it . . . I failed this badly . . . for the spell to backfire this much," I stuttered.

"No." Magoo's single word made me spin in shock, still shaken by what I witnessed.

"You cast the spell perfectly. You are a prodigy, after all," he repeated.

"Then . . . why? WHY? That spell was meant to heal!" I was becoming slightly hysterical.

"You naïve boy. You think a little green light and some special words will solve all your problems? Those will do nothing, NOTHING, if you don't understand what you are doing properly! Listen here and listen closely, the words tempus fugit . . . they are in a language that came from a time even before the age of the Ancients! They mean *time flies*. So, the spell that all those foolish priests use to 'heal' injuries does little more than speed up how the body naturally deals with said injuries," Magoo explained.

I still could not stop shaking uncontrollably. "Then, if the wound is life threatening . . ."

"Then 'healing magic' will have the opposite effect and will kill the subject faster, as well as be much more painful. I may not be entirely sure, but I think it's probably the worst possible way to go . . . to die from the inside out," Magoo spoke gravely.

"Why?" I continued to mutter. "Why couldn't you just tell me? For any living being to have to go through this . . ."

"This lesson isn't something you can fully understand the consequences of if I just tell you. If I just tell you not to do something, you'd still consider the possibility, still be desperate enough to try it, and still might try to make the same mistakes I once made."

I fell to my knees, unable to say another word.

"Most magic is all about performing a specific action. And actions have consequences. Always." Magoo continued. "If you're that desperate to save a life, then make an effort to not let danger approach others in the first place. Because the lesson in this is . . ." Magoo looked at the steaming remains of the animal again. "Desperation is wasted after the deed is already done."

My shock finally broke into sadness. I cried at what I had done.

"I'll be waiting in the shack when you're ready for the next lesson." And he left me there.

⤴

The small porch on his shack is where he was waiting for me the next day. He tossed some cashews he must've picked from woodland edge into his mouth. "Huh, so you really came back . . . usually by now, my student would quit. Now that you know the truth of the trade, do you still want to continue pursuing studying magic?"

I was silent, still trying to organize my thoughts after what had I witnessed. And I was trying to rub away my streams of tears.

"You remember that line I gave you earlier? The limits of your magic and the limits of your imagination are one and the same. That holds true for whatever sick and depraved ideas we people can think up, and the human imagination is a boundless thing. It's why mage craft is not quite glamourous as some make it out to be. Sights like that are common." Magoo kept tossing cashews in his mouth.

To say my enthusiasm for learning magic wasn't curbed after seeing that would be a big lie, however . . .

"Back at the deer . . . you said to make an effort to save others before it's too late right?"

"And? What of it?"

My right hand, which cast the spell was still shaking, but my left I balled into a fist. *That's right,* I thought to myself, *I can't forget why I'm doing this in the first place! I need to strengthen my resolve!* "You can teach me, right? How I can use power to protect others! If something that terrible can be done with magic, then I can create something equally as wonderful. I want to learn how to do it . . . and shape my own future!"

Magoo's complexion broke into a huge grin. I've never seen him smile like that before, and it was a large contrast to angry scowl from earlier. "Let's begin! The second lesson starts now!"

The intense training regimen began anew and went back to Magoo pummeling the crap out of me. But as the training went on, I found myself much more focused. It wasn't as if I learned any new spells or anything, more like I understood how each spell had its strengths and weaknesses and which other spells could make up for said weaknesses. What I learned from my horrible mistake was that every spell had to be practical, a small solution to the specific problem I was facing. If Magoo used ice mage, melt it with fire. If Magoo used an electrical spell, grow an insulator out of plant life. He also didn't seem to half-ass his spells from a distance anymore, instead working on combing his spells, one after another in order to subdue me. I saw how he picked up the pace and matched his combos. It went on like that for a while.

"Hmmm? No hesitation with the plant magic? Surely you realize it's the same type of magic like the healing spell?" Magoo inquired.

"Yeah," I muttered through heavy breathes.

"But you still use it to protect yourself?"

"Others die so that I can live; it's true for the vegetables and meat I eat in order to survive; the circle of life, no?"

"Oho! You're more mature than I thought! Try something else for me: grow an orange tree."

I did as he instructed. In a couple of seconds, one sprouted from the ground in front of me, starting from a sapling to a small tree, gaining more and more branches till it bore fruit.

Magoo plucked one of the oranges off it and tossed it over to me. "Try it."

I peeled off the skin and ate a piece, instantly spitting it out. It tasted absolutely rancid.

Magoo cackled at the sight of me disgusted with my tongue refusing to enter back in my mouth. "Well? How's it taste?" He asked in a gloating fashion.

"It tafes like my tongue hafes me now."

My response made Magoo cackle with laughter even harder. "Moreover, have you noticed your tree?"

I looked over at the tree, which was starting to wither and decay. "It happens slower with plant life." Magoo explained. "But for the most part, it is the same as the deer. Growing a tree from little to nothing is a time spell too. That's the thing about magic: it is all *temporary*. All the strength of our creations, the things we grow, are all unnatural. An imitation of a real thing, so in time, whatever we make quickly fades into obscurity. It doesn't taste quite as good as a real orange, does it? However, there is one exception to this rule. You think you can guess what it is?"

"It is . . . I don't know."

"C'mon, guess!"

"Apocalyptic magic?"

"Righto! The one type of spell that's been attempted by every magician since magecraft was a thing! The one spell that could destroy civilizations as great as the Ancients! Yet no one has ever been able to perform anything of the like, myself included!"

"You want me to perform that big of a spell?" I asked, all nervous again.

"HA! You? Performing apocalyptic magic? That's a good laugh! You can't even perform cataclysmic magic yet! All you've been doing is slinging around basic spells willy nilly. I think it's high time we begin the second lesson: teaching you cataclysmic magic!"

"But I thought we already started the second lesson," I said, sheepishly.

"When?"

"Back when you said: 'the second lesson starts now!'" I mimicked Magoo's voice.

"Yeah, as in it starts now."

"Then what was that earlier?"

"Review."

"Review?" I asked, pained again.

"Yes."

These conversations with him seemed to get increasingly repetitive as well as exhausting.

Chapter Twenty-One
Resolve Strengthened

THE SECOND LESSON DID, IN FACT, NOT START NOW AS MAGOO claimed it would. Instead, we started travelling once more. We packed up the shack and continued due south through the nation of Syracoosa. The scenery changed from dangerous forests to nice relaxing yellow plains. Seldom few moments were we ever attacked by any creatures, and when we did, it was mostly a small animal. Magoo would mutter something about moving quickly, as if it was too boring here.

I welcomed the change of pace compared to the ghoulish training earlier. The villages around here were welcoming and had good food. Apparently, they had an impressive capital further south, but we didn't get the chance to see it, mostly because Magoo kept going on about how this wasn't a damn sightseeing trip, and I should pay more attention to our surroundings.

He said that, but along the whole trip, I saw him writing letters to someone. Upon my noticing, he often hid them away from me, and whenever I ended up asking him about it, he very swiftly retorted something along the lines of "mind yer own business!" or "what's it to you?" I ended up dropping the matter, it wasn't as if he could find any time to deliver them anyway.

We changed directions and started moving east after gathering supplies from one more town. This part was a long stretch in our voyage, trekking many days and nights through the plains of Syracoosa. There were a few rural farms here and there, but for the most part, the stretch of land held no towns and villages, at least none that held anyone still alive.

One day, we ended up seeing it. In the distance, we could make out one of the now abandoned city of Ancients. The structures were made of a particularly smooth type of grey stone, strangely cube-like, and incredibly tall, much taller than any castle I'd ever seen. It was very unusual to see a structure so towering; it cast a striking contrast against the very flat plains. And what's more is that most of the building seemed partially collapsed, so what I was seeing wasn't even their actual height. As the two of us got closer, we could see that vines overgrew the buildings, as well as the strange four-legged metal beasts that lay dormant in the city's streets. Not a single creature stirred or made a noise in the entire place, which made the town increasingly eerie.

"Weird, huh?" Magoo broke the silence.

"Yeah, why doesn't this settlement have any walls?" I replied.

"Probably because I don't think they needed it. Wars were not as frequent in the time of the Ancients; most of their nations lived through enough of them to realize the futility. Plus, even though none of them had any access to magic whatsoever, they were still capable of flight. They could it by making these winged metal contraptions, much like those things over there." He motioned to one the sleeping metal things.

"The Ancients could fly?"

"Oh yes, their civilization was much more advanced than ours. They had a better understanding of the world than you or I, boy." Magoo looked strangely reminiscent of the place around him.

Now that I thought about it, our journey through the plains wasn't exactly completely straight. At first, I believed it could have been so that we see those villages to resupply every now and then.

But I had a sneaking suspicion Magoo wanted to show me this place.

Suddenly, Magoo froze. I also realized we weren't alone anymore. In the silent city, the slight sound of squishy noises came from the ruins of a weirdly hourglass-shaped building, and then *it* came into view. Across one of the streets, a small green gelatinous ooze was slowly but surely inching its way toward us. The old man immediately backed away, and I burst into laughter. Seeing Magoo so afraid of the tiny slimeball was hilarious.

"W-why are you laughing?" he said, backing away from it.

"Cause, it's just a slime!"

"Don't you 'it's just a slime' me!" He imitated my voice badly. "That *thing* is dangerous! Might be worse than dragons!"

"Aren't they supposed to be one the weakest monsters out there?"

"What on earth could give you such a ridiculous notion?"

As if to prove his point, a small rabbit which must've came from outside the city made the mistake of scurrying slightly too close to the slime. In one motion, the slime swallowed the rabbit, dissolving its fur, flesh, bones, and all till it was nothing. What's more was the slime was see through, allowing Magoo and I to clearly see the rabbit being digested. I jumped back, stunned. It grew in size a tad and continued inching toward the both of us.

Wide-eyed, I threw spells at it. Fireballs bounced off it. Lightning could only create a small fizzle on its surface. I tried to freeze it; all that did was change its color from green to turquoise. Nothing I threw at it made a difference. It just kept sluggishly inching its way to me, undeterred. I looked behind me, and Magoo was gone.

"Eh?" Making the same noise my mentor made, I scoured the area, looking for him. A brief moment later, I saw him running at full speed away from the creature down the opposite street. And, oh my, was it a sight to see. That feeble old man suddenly became an athletic sprinter. I could hardly keep up with him.

"Wait-for-me!" I breathed, following behind him.

"No! I'mnotgonnagooutbeingslimebait!"

After putting some distance between us and the thing, we caught our breath.

"Why'd-you-leave-me?" I panted.

"It would take a coordinated effort between skilled magicians to bring down a monster as tough as a slime, young'in." Magoo was coughing. "Their one and only weakness is that they can't move that fast, so they tend to stay in one area. It's probably why there are no animals in this city. They've all been gobbled up by that slime and any else that might be here."

I kept breathing hard.

"Just be glad it wasn't a mimic slime. Those buggers *become* whatever attacks them." Magoo continued. "A nightmare dealin with those."

Having successfully put the danger behind us, and the two of us still being on guard, we marveled at the metropolis until we reached its end. Even though the place was much more massive than any city I'd ever seen, Magoo told me by the ancient's standards the place we passed through was relatively small, and most likely it was only part of a ruined city. With the rest of it either underground or swept away by some disaster. After passing through the town of the Ancients, we continued our trek through the plains, and the long journey gave me a chance to reflect.

A civilization as great as the Ancients, destroyed by the only apocalyptic spell . . .

∽

It took a small eternity to reach the end of those plains. When we finally did, I nearly broke down from exhaustion. Weeks on end we did very little but march through, only stopping for sleep, Magoo forced me to eat while walking. We were out of Syracoosa by now, the never-ending plains now gave way to rock, mountainous terrain. Magoo tells me by now we've reached a nation called Geese.

"Geese? Like the bird?"

"Yeah, like the bird."

"Why name a nation after a bird?"

"Why'd the hell would I know?" Magoo snapped back, irritated with my questions. "Hurry up, I wanna climb this mountain before noon!" He pointed at the tallest one in sight.

Of course it'd be the tallest one, I thought to myself. Already exhausted from the long trek, I pushed through and managed to crawl up to the top of the peak. I lay down on the hard rock. Everything was sore or hurting afterward, and I could barely move a muscle.

"Great, now we begin," said Magoo.

"Huh?"

I took me another second to realize that what he meant was that he was starting the second lesson now.

"Wai—" I panicked. He made short work of me. I got up quickly to deflect some spells, but my defense was pathetic. In no time at all, I was blasted back to laying down on the hard rock.

"Wait?" Magoo scoffed. "Enemies aren't going to wait till you're at your best lad. If anything, the more dangerous ones will wait till you're at your worst."

He had a point there.

"It takes stamina to cast magic, as I'm sure you're aware. And you've got little to none of it!" He pointed his finger at me, who was busy panting on the ground. "I outran you back there at the slime! You couldn't even keep up with an old ailing man, which is why I brought you here. To get some proper exercise!"

For the next month and a half, he made me sprint up and down that mountain. All the while he shot spells at me to keep me on my toes. For the most part, I leapt from stone to stone to avoid him. But the explosive spells and falling boulders that I had to avoid seemed a little excessive for an exercise. The seventy-degree incline and thin mountain air made the training very grueling indeed, but toward the end of it, I finally built up an "adequate amount of stamina" as Magoo described it.

"Now, another difference between basic and cataclysmic magic beside scale is also the words needed to activate the spell. Basic magic has only one or two words at most, and cataclysmic magic requires to chant a whole verse in order to activate. It's what any normal magic professor would teach; however, that is also very foolish!" said Magoo smugly.

"Why?"

"Why?" Magoo poorly imitated me again. "Because no enemy in their right mind is just going to wait for you to read a poem to them in the middle of freakin combat, yougoshdarncrustylobster!"

Did he just call me a lobster?

"If you wanna be a mage, boy . . ." Magoo put his hand to the stone ground. All around me, the stone ground cracked, then broke, reforming itself into multiple humanoid shapes. I found myself surrounded by multiple stone mannequins around me. Magoo was going all out.

". . . then you might as well become a great mage. A great mage can handle himself and doesn't need protection from others to cast spells." Magoo gave a nefarious grin, and I was set upon by the mannequins.

It was practically impossible to maintain a distance from them. The mannequins dodged to and fro and either moved under my guard or tried to jump on top of me. I responded with bursts of fire and ice, stopping just a few, but the rest just kept coming at me. I understood what I had to do; the answer was staring at me in the face. If basic magic could be used without a command word, then it should be the same for cataclysmic magic. Magoo must've wanted me to blast these mannequins apart with a cataclysmic spell. However, they weren't giving me so much as a second to think.

Ducking punches, breaking out of sudden grabs from behind, and avoiding their acrobatic spin attacks, I could just make barely keep up! That was until out of nowhere, a bolt of purple hit me from the side. The mannequins got a hold of me, and I was immobilized. I looked up and saw Magoo, his right hand looked like he was controlling the mannequins like a puppeteer, but his left hand was completely free, and pointing at me as if he just fired that last spell.

"Hmmm, not quite there yet, eh boy?" Magoo's puppeteering hand scrunched up into a fist, and all the mannequins crumbled away. "You didn't even pay attention to your opponent," he said, shaking his head in disappointment.

I was beet red. I got so wrapped up avoiding the mannequins I just let Magoo do whatever he wished. And it became devastatingly clear how much the skill difference was between us was. I mean, I knew he was a powerful grandmaster, but controlling a small legion of stone golems with ease, while still firing off unique magic that I've never seen before, was just ridiculous. Not only that, but each stone golem he summoned moved with the precision and skill of a veteran soldier.

"Welp, no matter! You'll just have to try again beating me tomorrow!" he said matter-of-factly. "Just remember, you can do this! The limits of your magic and the limits of your imagination are one and the same."

The next day went by in a similar fashion. I actually paid attention to the spells that Magoo would fire off while dodging the mannequins, but it wasn't as if I could avoid all of them. What's more was the mannequins that Magoo summoned in seemed to be improving against me! As I tried to freeze one, another knocked me off protecting his fellow mannequin! They developed counters to my counters and kept the pressure on me fiercely to jump on whatever opening Magoo created.

"If you can't outlearn a bunch of rocks, then I don't know what to tell you, boy." Magoo gloated, as I was pinned by his army again.

It was as embarrassing as it was irritating. I was mostly frustrated with myself for not seeing a way to beat the mannequins.

Magoo sighed. "Fine then, guess I'll give you a hint. Why do mages keep their distance?"

"In order to gain the advantage . . ." I trailed off. Wait, is it an advantage though? When mages back off, the further the distance usually means the more reaction time given to the enemy to dodge or block the spells that are casted. Getting closer to your opponent gives a higher chance to land the spell! The only reason to back off would be because usually mages are weak at hand-to-hand fighting, but that doesn't necessarily need to be true. If I could learn to fight hand to hand, while incorporating magic, I could turn my biggest weakness into a strength!

"I'll leave you to it," he said, seeing me deep in thought.

It took many more tries against Magoo's onslaught of rock men for me to defeat them. I trained my stamina in order to cast more spells, but it would take training to my physique to give me more opportunities to cast them. I didn't have any weapons to practice with, but that should be fine since the mannequins were unarmed as well. So, after every failed attempt, I took the opportunity to train by myself for the rest of the day. I incorporated kicks, acrobatic stunts, martial arts, whatever I could find buried in Magoo's library into my magic to become a force to be reckoned with. Until one day, after I don't know how many tries, I rose to challenge Magoo once more.

"Well, well . . . twentieth times the charm huh?" Magoo coughed.

I stood opposite of him, prepared. The ground around me began to crack once more. He held out his puppeteering hand and took some pot shots with his other hand right at the start. I deflected the spells and turned to the mannequins. I breathed hard, but I was fully focused. The first mannequin came at me, and I solidified rocks from the ground around my hand like a glove and

punched it, obliterating it and my glove to pieces. A second
mannequin came behind me. I used the rocks from my shattered
makeshift glove to orbit around me to gain momentum and slam
into the mannequin. Magoo took another shot at me, and I dodged.
The surrounding mannequins became more vicious, and I
responded in turn. Dispatching them one by one, I slowly but
surely made my way toward Magoo. After freezing and blasting
apart about six of them, I broke through their ranks and attacked
him. He chuckled, apparently impressed that I could get that close
to him. He responded by flinging more spells my way, and in the
small distance between us, the ground began to crack again. He was
summoning more of those mannequins!

"Hey! That ain't fair!" I shouted through the spells.

"Since when is a fight ever fair?" he chuckled.

Things looked to be getting rough for me. Eliminating all the
mannequins before taking Magoo on was no longer an option.
Summoning the reserves of my energy, I put on a burst of extra
speed, dashing through the mannequins that he just summoned,
dodging them but not bothering to counterattack. Getting
uncomfortably close to Magoo, he put his guard up in
preparation of my next spell. I've planned for this, for the
moment I could break away from the mannequins. I probably
wouldn't have multiple chances to attack Magoo with spells; he
definitely wouldn't leave me that many openings, so the use of
basic magic to attack him was not an option. Therefore, I needed
to use the goal of my training: cataclysmic magic.

Already tired, but not deterred, I leaped in the air above
Magoo. The air above him and around me cooled and mist shot out
of my hands. The vapors began to crystalize in an instant, rapidly
freezing an area as large as the mountain's peak. It was my very first
cataclysmic spell which I studied, a high-level ice spell. I summoned
a huge glacier and threw it at my wide-eyed teacher. The crackle of
the ice hitting the peak that we were on caused multiple echoes in

the mountainous landscape around us. The glacier broke apart on top of the mountain, causing a small avalanche. The spell I unleashed deposited a thick layer of snowfall and ice on the rocky terrain, effectively burying Magoo and all the mannequins.

Pleased with my work, I stood on top of the snowy pile, exhausted. A sheet of white now covered the over-frozen mountain top. A couple seconds passed, then a minute, and nothing happened. "Oh shit," I whispered. I took it way too far! I frantically dug at the melting snow with my hands. I had just buried a feeble old man under a freakin' avalanche. What in the world was wrong with me? A couple meters behind my frantic digging, Magoo's head and only his head popped out of the snow. I breathed in a sigh of relief.

He was laughing and looked like the first flower of spring growing out of the snow like that. "A glacier, huh? Well done, kid. I didn't expect it." He chuckled giving a big old smile. I was reminded of the stark contrast of how he was when I first met him.

"I guess a congratulations are in order for you, boy," he said while I dug him out of the snow. "You pass."

"Huh? I passed what?"

"My last test of course! Now I have taught you all you need to know in order to become a *great* mage!"

"Wait, your last test? So, we just spent two years travelling for only two lessons?"

"Eh?" he made the goat noise again. "Don't take my lessons so lightly boy! The fact that it took you two years alone to even learn them is proof enough of how important and strenuous they are!"

"O-of course!" I replied, apologizing for my rudeness.

Magoo sighed. "You were right to be suspicious though, so let me rephrase what I said earlier. Listen kid, that is the final lesson that you will receive from me. What I just taught you is not the end all be all of what you will do with your magic. What I did was teach you how to learn magic, which is something you will most likely do by yourself. One never stops learning in their lifetime."

"Then, that's it? Our journey is over?" I had to admit, I felt a little sad. I've gotten to like the old codger.

I think Magoo might have noticed me slightly downcast. "Well, now we can start to celebrate! After all, you're my only student to have passed my tests! I am proud of ya, kid."

That night, in a shack precariously somehow nesting on top of a mountain, we celebrated. It was a big feast for just the two of us, although it wasn't exactly lonely. With Matthew and mannequins wandering about, it was a very grand party. We enjoyed ourselves thoroughly, casting joke spells at each other, and laughing the night away.

"Say, what if we sent a letter to your parents?" Magoo sprung me the question out of nowhere.

"What for?"

"Don't you want to let them know of your promising progress? Also, they seem like good folk from when I met them in Angrost, I bet they might be worried of their son. I've already been sending them my own updates, though I'm sure they'd rather hear from you."

"Huh? Why didn't you ask me about this earlier?"

"Cause, knowing you, you'd lose even more focus than usual on your training. But I also don't want there to be any more rumors going around saying I abducted you away or anything!" The way he said that made it look like he was trying to keep up his grumpy persona. When I met him around the outskirts of Angrost, I didn't think of him the type to care much about rumors.

"Sure, I think writing a letter is a great idea."

"Of course, it is! I came up with it after all!" His smug attitude never changed.

We spent the night each writing to my folks. I put everything that had happened in my letter. I wanted my parents to see every amazing thing I saw and just how much I missed them. When my fingers finally stopped moving my quill, I looked over to Magoo to see how his letter was coming along.

He shielded his parchment with his hand. "No peeking."

"Aww, c'mon! I'll show you mine!"

"No!"

I kept pestering him, while he furiously scribbled faster. Matthew, who was relaxing near a chair suddenly wrapped around my head, covering my eyes. By the time I finally wrestled him off, Magoo finished his letter.

"Ha! I win again!"

"I still beat you in training!" I pouted.

"Yeah, only after I whooped yer skinny little hide twenty times over! Hehe . . ."

Magoo then took both of our letters, folded them up and put them in an envelope. He then cast a spell on the envelope, which seemed to fold in on itself, growing wings and flew out the window. That was another unique spell I hadn't seen before. I looked at Magoo in skepticism.

"What?" he said looking guilty. "Gotta keep some secrets to myself!"

We both laughed and enjoyed the rest of the night. The envelope however, had a far more perilous journey than ours, heading straight for the capital city of Pravah, Angrost.

Chapter Twenty-Two
Suspicions Confirmed

IT WAS ONLY THROUGH A SPARSE FEW TRUSTED SOURCES THAT I learned of the events which happened in the capital of Pravah while I left the country. Namely, most of the information I received came from the King's son, Reginold the Second, who used to be an old childhood friend. It was not uncommon for the King's child to play with the sons and daughters of nobles. He and I hit it off and became rather good buddies when we were both toddlers. But still, I was a child of a nobleman, and as soon as my father started to lose popularity in court, the two of us became distant friends. And when I decided to pursue studying magic, we stopped meeting altogether.

My father, Isaac, also had friends of his own. It was an especially important thing to have friends in high places as a nobleman. Although as he began to lose popularity in court and was branded with the unfortunate nickname of the Pauper, most of those friends all but vanished. Nearly all the noblemen distanced themselves from Isaac, lest they get my father's criticisms come their way. The only one who decided to remain close to him despite the many insults was a Franch nobleman named Pierre. Pierre Wallenhaus was a nobleman of Pravah who happened to be born from the neighboring nation of Frant to the west. He would often serve as an intermediate or as an emissary between the two nations. Even still, he was considered a foreigner by most in the court, so having much in common with my father, he and the Pauper were great friends.

"So, that son of yours left the capital, eh?" Pierre started one morning. He spoke in the usual accent of someone from the nation of Frant.

He was visiting Isaac in my father's private studies early one morning, which was actually just a couple boxes arranged in the court's cellar with the smaller box being used as a chair and the larger box being the table. An oil lamp with a quill and ink sat on the larger box, and a mess of papers were strewn about the place. They ranged from the court's orders on arrested criminals within the city, to building rights, to tax collection from villages within Pravah, it seemed as though everything happening in the nation was going through that cellar.

"Oh, erm, did I come at a bad time?" said Pierre, looking around and finding no trace of Isaac within the mountains of parchment.

"Ah, Pierre!" said a voice. Peeking out from one of the more particularly tall stacks of documents was Isaac. "I'm afraid there isn't too many good times to come in, but you're always welcome here." He was desperately trying to organize the disarray of papers to little to no avail. Isaac looked like he hadn't left the cellar in quite a while. His hair was greasy and unkept, and dark circles under his eyes showed that he hadn't slept for a while either.

"Are you all right?" Pierre felt the need to ask.

"Positively swamped. They got me doing the work from some of the other court officials' jurisdictions. Otherwise, I'm fine. You know, when I got into this job, I'd thought there would be more cocktail dinner parties than paperwork." Isaac said this while juggling documents that were on the verge of spilling over in his hands.

"And how's Frank and Lisandra?" Pierre caught the papers from his hands.

"Lisandra's okay as well, bet she's frustrated being out of the loop and all, but I think she understands. Frank has gone all gung-ho saying he'll be the next court mage or something and went off with that new teacher of his. Man, I don't even know where they went. What kind of parent am I?"

"Don't beat yourself up about it too much."

"Think he's starting to see how my work might be getting to me. Kid's too darn perceptive and likes sticking his nose into things that get him into trouble."

"Sounds a lot like someone I know."

Isaac opened his mouth as if he was going to say something, then thought against it. He put down all of the files he was juggling.

"So, think you could use a hand?" Pierre looked at Isaac desperately trying to organize the disaster and was handing Isaac papers as he found them.

"What? You free right now?"

"Well, no. But, c'mon, you gotta let me at least try to lighten your load. It hurts to look at you."

"Gee . . . thanks."

"Isaac!"

"All right, all right." Issac sighed. "There is this one case I've been putting off, seems sort of dangerous. There's apparently a large group of insurgents organizing somewhere to the east, can't pin their exact location."

"A large group of bandits?"

"What I thought at first, but then a couple of insurgency leaders were spotted here in the capital a few days back, so it seems like something much more serious. I think they were seen leaving with carts of something. We have reason to suspect they might have a spy somewhere here in Angrost. Are you sure you want to take this assignment? The guard detail that spotted these guys were heavily injured, they're all in Angrost's general hospital."

"Relax, I'll be fine! All I will do is ask some questions and point the guards in the right direction. I can also put up a job for one of the adventurer guilds; there's no need for me to be in harm's way."

"If you say so. Do be careful." Isaac handed Pierre all the documents he had on the matter, and Pierre departed for the hospital.

☙

It was midafternoon around the time Pierre reached the hospital. The streets around the place seemed deserted, hard to imagine that there were critically injured guards inside. When he did enter, he was met with an unwelcome surprise in the lobby of the building.

"Hmmm? Pierre, nice to see you here this fine day."

"I wish I could say the same, Montegew. But that would be another bold-faced lie." Pierre's tone was a mix of sarcasm and disgust.

"A bold-faced lie? Whatever could you mean? I assure you, I am extraordinarily happy to see such an esteemed colleague as yourself here on this nice day. You're here to see the guards that were injured just yesterday, right? I'd be more than willing to help accompany you."

"I'd rather you didn't."

"Nonsense! I insist," said Montegew, already leading Pierre to place where the guards were.

Pierre hated the very notion of having to be led by Montegew, but the quicker he could finish Frank's assignment, the quicker he would be rid of this charlatan. Then, Montegew could inconvenience the next nobleman and would leave Pierre to finish his tasks. Pierre knew Montegew wasn't the most entrusted individual in the court by far, but it would be easier to pretend to get along.

"So, what are you doing here? I didn't think you were part of this case," Pierre asked, walking through the halls with Montegew.

"Oh, I had meetings with a few business associates of mine. I believe the injured guards might have information on the goods that were taken from the capital."

"You knew what goods were stolen? I thought from the reports that was unconfirmed."

"They were unconfirmed, yes of course. I made further investigations into the matter myself, much like what you are up to now, I presume? Ah, well, I suppose we have to cut our conversations short, for here we are."

They both stopped in front of the door that led to the guard's chambers.

"After you." Montegew said, smiling and holding the door open for Pierre.

Pierre shook his head in disapproval but continued in anyway. Only when he entered in further could he see the grim sight set before him. All the guards from the incident were dead. Killed in the very beds they were resting; pools of blood covered the floor. The people who stood above them, with bloodied weapons in hand, were members of the insurgents, only identified from the rough sketches of the reports Isaac handed to him. A sharp pain pierced Pierre, looking down he saw his own abdomen, spilling with blood. He fell over. The door closed behind him, and he looked over to see Montegew with a bloodied dagger in his hands.

"The spy . . . it was you . . ." Pierre croaked.

Montegew chuckled. "*A* spy." He corrected him. "Now you know why I was so happy to see you today."

Pierre lost consciousness.

⤵

Isaac was at the time, still busy in the cellar. The workload was considerably lighter now that Pierre took away the job that looked like the most trouble, but he still couldn't help but feel guilty leaving it to Pierre just like that. He'd have to treat him to food and a drink in the Spittoon later.

The cellar was quiet save for the sound of Isaac's quill scratching at the many parchments. Minutes passed, then hours. His work was then interrupted by the cellar door slamming open and armed guards pouring in. They aimed their spears at the startled man sitting by the boxes.

"Isaac Olsenhein, you are accused for subvert actions against the crown, and are to report to the high court immediately. You are also to put these on." One of the guards handed Isaac restraints.

"Subvert actions? I have never once shown a disloyalty to this nation! I demand to know what I am accused of!" Isaac expression was grim. *Was this another vie for power?* It looked like the work of Montegew.

The guard stepped forward, angry, and put the chains on Isaac himself. "You are accused of the death of one Pierre Wallenhaus."

"Pierre is dead?" Isaac said meekly, most of his earlier outrage draining away for sorrow upon hearing that his best friend had just been killed. He allowed himself to get taken and led away.

How was he dead? Pierre was just with me earlier today . . . He thought to himself.

Isaac then came to the stark conclusion that Pierre died while on the assignment he just handed him. That one job that he didn't make the time for got someone else hurt. Isaac got hit full force with the crushing guilt of getting his best friend killed.

He hung his head in shame and resentment. He was led in that manner, all the way to the court, before King Reginold. News of Pierre's death was spread quickly among the noblemen, and all of them were present. Some of them were summoned before the King; others reported in right away as soon as they heard the tragedy. All were present to bear witness as Isaac, my father, was led in chains before the leaders of the nation.

"Isaac Olsenhein, you stand accused of the murder of Pierre

Wallenhaus, an invaluable servant to Pravah, as well as conspiracy against the court and royal family." One squire read off Isaac's charges. "Count Montegew will represent the prosecution in the following proceedings, as he is the official who happened to be investigating a related matter."

Isaac, while still in chains and surrounded by guards, knelt before Reginold the First. He didn't look up but knew that the King had a look of disgust written across his face. Isaac wanted nothing more but to take the time to grieve for his lost friend but that would have to wait until he could find Pierre's killer. And even that would have to wait before Isaac could clear the suspicions on himself, it was severely unfortunate that his prosecutor had to be that man of all people. Too many thoughts swam around Isaac's head, all the while Montegew put on a spectacular show for the audience of noblemen.

"Pierre Wallenhaus, an invaluable member of this great court, was found dead this afternoon by a stab wound in the back inside Angrost's general hospital. He was found like this next to several more dead men, who were the guards who were admitted into the hospital just two days ago. The very same guards who valiantly defended this city from would-be aggressors, we let die within our very walls!" Montegew's voice echoed throughout the walls of the court.

All the spectators began to murmur amongst themselves as they learned of Pierre's death. Montegew waited for the noise from the audience to die down before continuing.

"For these 'insurgents,' as we call them, to get away with this offence is unacceptable. And would be impossible if it not for this fact: gentlemen, we have a spy planted among us." Montegew paused for moment, waiting for the shocked gasps from the court to subside.

"Going forward, we should not show arrogance in thinking these dangerous individuals as insurgents, but as a militant faction, and a possible coup to overthrow our illustrious king. Now more than ever, our duties as noblemen of the nation of Pravah are clear; to serve the King, and to serve this nation. We will rise to this issue to protect our people and our kingdom!"

Montegew's speech was met with applause.

After the applause died down Montegew continued. "My friends, now we must address the uncomfortable issue of a traitor in our midst. To give a clear picture of what had transpired this day, I will go over the evidence that was found on Pierre's body. THIS NOTE!" Montegew held up a court order to hunt down insurgents organizing in the east, part of the documents Isaac handed to Pierre before his death. It was covered in splotches of blood.

"This order was a call for investigation or suppression of the very insurgents who killed Mr. Wallenhaus, and it came from the desk of none other than Isaac Olsenhein!" He pointed an accusatory finger at the man in chains. "We also have interviewed some of the cleaning staff, who confirm that the last man Pierre Wallenhaus visited before departing to the hospital was in fact Isaac Olsenhein! Under these points of interest, I urge the court to pursue the possibility that Mr. Olsenhein is a spy, and that he should be executed."

"Well, Isaac?" King Reginold finally spoke. "Is what he said true?"

There was a hushed silence in court, and whispered murmurs died down for the King's question to be answered.

"My king . . . I cannot apologize enough for my transgressions. My ignorance in this matter is unforgivable, and I've failed this nation. It is true that I met with Pierre before this incident, and that I handed him that document, a job which was assigned to me and no one else." As Isaac spoke, he looked down, partly in shame, partly to conceal his outrage.

"Even so," Isaac continued, "I did not partake in any action to harm Pierre, nor any action against this country. I only ask for a chance of redemption, to find the one responsible for this, and to better serve this nation."

Isaac looked in skepticism at Montegew.

Montegew flashed back a smile.

"Very well," the King stood and all in the court followed suite. "I have heard both cases and will now pass judgement. I decree that Isaac Olsenhein is found guilty of aiding and hiding rebellious forces to the nation of Pravah. However, considering his long devotion to Pravah and extended history of accomplishments, I move that he be spared of execution. He will remain in the capital, imprisoned and unable to leave, continuing his duties. He will also be kept under strict surveillance. That is all. This court is now adjourned."

Everyone in the audience, noblemen and all, filed away, outside of the court, leaving behind only the King, Isaac, and the few guards who would take him away.

"Why would you do this to me, Isaac? I can understand you're frustrated in court, but to take up arms against me? You really are no longer the friend I once knew," Reginold said sadly. He frowned and shook his head in pity at his old friend. He looked like he wanted to say more but decided against it.

"I would never even dream of doing something like that. And I would never harm Pierre. You should know that he and I were close. Montegew knows something about his death that he doesn't want to share. That man is playing you for a fool."

"I am no fool."

"That's not what I meant—let me rephrase. That man's deceitful and cunning. He's trying to pin all of this as my doing while he prepares his own plans. Most likely he is the one who is the spy."

Reginold shook his head. "So, this really is just another vie for power between the two of you. And here I thought that you of all people would be more graceful in defeat."

"This is no vie for power, but the beginnings of a coup against you! Montegew's planning to undermine you. Maybe even take control of Pravah!"

"And what evidence do you have of this?"

Isaac's frantic words suddenly stopped short, "None. But I can tell he wants me out of the way of what he plans next."

Reginold shook his head in pity for the man in front of him. "He has plenty of evidence on you, though."

"Please be careful around him." Isaac pleaded.

"I will take no advice from an enemy spy. There's no merit in your words if I can't tell they're true."

"There would be no merit even if they were true! By the time my words are confirmed, it will be too late!" yelled Isaac. His frustration was written upon the grim expression on his face, and he shouted to make his outrage show.

"THAT'S ENOUGH!" Reginold boomed. "Take him out of my sight!" he ordered his guards.

～

Secretly, off to the side, away from the prying eyes of the court and King, three men meet in secret. They were just outside Angrost's keep, and it was below the pitch black of night. Under the hooded disguises were Count Montegew, Duke Jeffery, and one more whose face was obscured. The third member of the party was unidentifiable, looked like more of a shadow than a man.

"Is it really all right to meet in the open like this?" said Jeffery.

"Yes, it's quite all right. Motions are underway now that can't be stopped, the plan is moving along swimmingly." Montegew replied.

"And? What of the slight problem? You know, the one we'd said we'd address?"

"Well, that's why I brought along our silent friend here with us."

"Is it really all right for him to be here of all places?"

"Of course, he is a professional. Leaving this place unseen should be a cakewalk for someone of his caliber. Jeffery, I'd for you to meet Mr. Rolan. He'll be the one taking care of our worries for us, won't you Mr. Rolan?"

The shadow nodded. In his clutches was an envelope with folded wings, struggling to escape.

Chapter Twenty-Three
A Chance Encounter

I, OF COURSE, HAD NO CLUE OF WHAT WAS HAPPENING IN THE capital, far away from my secluded mountain top with Magoo. The morning after our celebratory party, Magoo packed up the shack one last time. And we said our goodbyes.

"Well, kid, it's been a pleasure." Magoo shook my hand.

"Thanks, a lot."

There was an uneasy silence around us until Magoo broke it again.

"I know you want to go back home as quickly as possible kid, but as it stands, I'd say you're still too inexperienced." Magoo said.

"Huh? But I thought you taught me everything I needed to know!"

"Everything that I could teach you, I taught you. But it is far from everything you need to know. The rest is up to you to learn on your own. Mage craft is a dangerous undertaking, and you might not figure out all of its secrets, but I know you'll go far, farther than what I could accomplish. I see that potential in you."

"But why can't I just continue learning in Angrost?"

"Because that city is full of exceptionally dangerous people. If you engage yourself in there as a mage and try to gain power in that court system of theirs now, you'll be snuffed out before you ever get the chance. You won't be treated like some starry-eyed child prodigy anymore lad; you'll be treated like a threat."

"I-I could take them, I've trained for this." Hearing Magoo talk about Angrost's court made me doubt if I really could take them.

Magoo sighed. "There's a reason you found me living outside that capital, Frank. Those people are cutthroat, and I'd rather not lose another promising student . . . Do you really want to take them on?"

"Yes."

Magoo sighed again. "Fine then, I'll help you. But only if you keep a promise for me. You break it, and that's it, you'll get nothing else from me."

"Okay."

"No, Frank. You *have* to keep this promise for me." Magoo put his arms on my shoulders and looked at me with a serious expression. That expression of his reminded me of the look he had on his face when I tried to heal the deer.

"Yes."

Magoo nodded. "One year. In one year, I'll meet you in Angrost. You must promise me not to go anywhere near the city till then."

"Okay."

"I wanna hear it."

"I promise not to go anywhere near Angrost for one year." I understood that Magoo's concerns were never without reason, and I trusted his judgement enough to keep this promise.

"Good. In one year, that will give you enough time to research and perfect your own magic the way that you want, so it's not just an imitation of mine. You'll become a great mage, I know it. And, as a parting gift, I can give you a piece of advice. For years on end, I devoted my life to attempting an Apocalyptic spell but never could. My theory was to incorporate the wisdom of the Ancients into my own magic. Use their knowledge, which they discovered with their science, and set it as a guideline for what magic could achieve. Their civilization was far greater that what ours has accomplished, but we can still catch up to them. Even though I may have failed, I still think it's a possibility for a mage to one day perform an Apocalyptic spell. Maybe it's something you could complete in your lifetime. I'd like for you to find the ruins of the Ancients, as many as you can within this one year, and learn all you can from people more capable than myself."

It was a big thing Magoo was entrusting to me, essentially his life's work. I vigorously nodded as he explained.

"It's a tough thing to learn, I heard the Ancients take years of their childhood life just to learn it. But you can do it in just one. You are a prodigy after all." Magoo grinned.

I gave him a hug, and he hugged me back.

"And make sure you remember that line I keep repeating at you." Magoo nagged.

"The limits of your magic and the limits of your imagination are one and the same," I said it like I was reading it off a book.

"HA! So, you do pay attention! But there's more to that saying than just improving your magic." Magoo drew close enough that I could see his wrinkled face. "The limits of your imagination and the limits of what you can accomplish are also one and the same."

He hugged me once more, and then, we parted ways off the mountain. I would not see him again for one year.

⌒

Magoo had left me with a daunting task ahead of me, to learn all I could of a civilization that has been forgotten by most. He left with me a map of all the ruins and areas which had Ancient architecture, but he warned me that it was only the places with known Ancient structures. I probably wouldn't find anything new or useful if I didn't try my hand at excavation. Either way, it would most likely be safer if I investigate the ruins on the map that he lent me first and decide for myself if there's any merit to them.

I set off on my journey, solo this time, heading northwest to a set of ruins that Magoo and I didn't pass by. I suspected he showed me all there is to know about that one. The ruins that I was after were buried somewhere to the west of the Rotten Forest, where the forest becomes not as rotten. It took me a couple weeks to backtrack the journey Magoo and I had taken together, but I moved fast thanks to my training. Navigating through the Rotten Forest became a breeze; it was hard to imagine I had difficulty traversing here when I began my journey with Magoo. The monsters of the forest didn't attack me quite as frequently, so maybe I was slightly stronger now.

Every time nightfall set, I readied up a small camp and cooked my meals. Without a nagging old man around me, it was quiet and a little lonely. I just ate in silence, slept, and then moved on. Nothing too remarkable. I repeated that process until I reached the western edge of the Rotten Forest.

With the old gray husks of wood behind me, the forest looked much different by comparison. For one, the trees had leaves upon their branches, but they were still wilting away. It appeared as though the place was in a perpetual state of autumn, even though at the time it was spring. And secondly, there was less of the trees themselves. The sparse placement of the trees allowed me to be able to see the sky over them, which wasn't something I could do in the center of the Rotten Forest, even if these trees had more leaves.

"Is this really the same forest?" I wondered aloud.

As I wandered through the forest's edge, farther in the distance, I could hear clanging. At first, I thought it was some creature I hadn't seen before from the forest. But as I grew closer to the sound, I couldn't mistake it for anything else; the sound of metal upon metal. Someone up ahead was crossing blades with another.

I started running toward the commotion. It was weird to meet someone in the Rotten Forest on account of how little people make it through the swampy marsh. If someone was under attack from one of the creatures of the forest, I needed to get there quickly to help. As the sound grew closer, I ran past more trees to a small clearing where I could see the culprit.

It wasn't any creature from the forest fighting. Instead, two people were crossing swords in the woodland. One was a knight donned in armor wielding a longsword in both his hands. He had a red plume in his helmet and was expertly deflecting the attacks of his aggressor with a solid stance, looking for any opening to inflict a jab on his opponent. His opponent, on the other hand, had anything but a solid stance. He was donned in leather armor and a dark red hood with a pitch-black helmet underneath. The armor he wore had spots of metal plating, which were mismatched. His left shoulder that had metal plating while the right did not. Similarly, his left hand had a metal gauntlet while his right was a leather glove. His whole attire looked like it would be hard to balance in a fight if it wasn't for his choice in weaponry. He wielded two blades; on his left he held a strangely short, curved knife. I think it was called a karambit, a weapon hailing from lands to the far east. On his right he held a great sword, a massive hunk of metal that was supposed to be wielded two-handed by warriors from the far northwest tribes he carried onehanded with ease.

The warrior in the dark hood had a fighting style that was a spectacle to behold. He was exceptionally light on his feet while wielding such a large blade, and every swing with that large sword that missed was used as momentum for his next swing. He twisted his body and span the sword in a full circle to land his next attack. He danced around the one in armor, harassing him with extremely fast jabs with his knife, changing his grip on the blade with every slice. The man was the personification of a spinning blade, although his movement and dark attire made him look more like a shadow than a man. The knight in armor could just about barely keep up with the knife, and still had the great sword to contend with; it was all too much, the one in armor was steadily losing ground.

Do I really have the right to break up this fight? Seeing these two skilled people locked in combat, it quickly put things into perspective. They looked to be intent on killing each other. I was reminded of that deer from this very forest and the resolution I made to Magoo to protect people. I became quickly aware of how difficult and maybe unrealistic such a dream was. Multiple decisions came at me in the second-by-second moment. *Do I help? Do I leave? Who would I save? And why?*

The knight was still standing, even if he was losing the battle against the shade. One of the shadow's large swings with the great sword came crashing in on the knight. The knight deflected the attack with the hilt of his longsword and a loud clang was heard. The knight pivoted, and in one swift motion brought his longsword downward with a thrust toward the shadow. In an even swifter motion, the shade deflected the thrust with his karambit. The small blade flicked the knight's thrust away from his midsection. The shadow kicked away from the knight and put them both off balance.

"Stop this! Now!" the knight exclaimed.

The shadow was quiet.

Then, as if unfazed, he dug his knife into the dirt ground for more traction, landing on his feet, and propelled himself at the knight. He was changing his momentum seamlessly, using his dagger to perfect his directions. The shadow's attacks, already extremely fast, grew even faster. His changing grips on his knife increased in speed and deadliness. He put more of his body behind his swings with the great sword. And he kept switching grips on his sword and knife between blows and swipes on a dime.

Overwhelming the knight, the shadow then unleashed his own thrust. The knight, seemingly on the verge of defeat, pivoted around his opponent's thrust. He used the moment to let loose a devastating swing with the longsword on his adversary's exposed back. In a split second, the shadow's karambit was already there, blocking his blow. The knife faced outwards and was hooked onto the longsword. The knight's defense was wide open. The shade stood before the knight, poised to end his life with his great sword.

Just before he could strike, I foolishly intervened. The great sword that was aimed for the knight's head instead embedded itself in a wall of ice. I erected it between the two and blocked the shadow's finishing strike.

My decision, I admit, was one not fully thought out. Or maybe something I couldn't properly express. Something vague, yet real. My point to try to protect people still seems unrealistic, more so now than ever. But I still wanted to make a proper attempt. So, the question to ask myself was this: at what point should you meddle in someone else's affairs? At what point should you help someone in need? At what moment does a stranger become a friend? At what moment does a stranger become an enemy? I could find no answer. So to me, that moment might as well be now. I made a choice to save the knight. Even if it isn't my business, I didn't want someone to die in front of me.

"What are you doing? Get out of here!" the knight yelled.

The shadow, upon noticing me, wasted no time at all. The blade was removed from the crumbling block of ice. He switched his target from the knight to me and traversed the distance between us in the blink of an eye. It was with sudden realization that I understood the one that needed saving was no longer the knight, but instead myself.

He swung his great sword at me. I ended up stopping the shadow's attack using my forearm encased in rocks, just like I used against Magoo's mannequins. But that was a terrible idea. The sheer force of his great sword's slash was too much. It felt as though my arm would get torn out of its socket. Had I used a slightly thinner layer of stones, my arm would've been lopped off.

That knight I just saved is able to parry these swings? I thought to myself.

The shadow faltered for less than half a second upon seeing me block his attack. I made the mistake of instinctively grabbing my arm in pain, and he let loose another finishing strike, this time upon myself. The knight rushed over and parried the shade's attack, pushing his swing to the ground directly right of me. The shadow retaliated with a spin, plunging his dagger at the knight. I quickly froze his left hand into a ball of ice, and his attack on the knight became more of a punch than a stab. He then kicked away from the knight and me.

The shadow breaking off his attack, if only for a moment, gave the knight and me a chance to catch our breaths. My guard still being up, I looked to the knight. Thankfully, I don't think he was all that badly injured from that shadow's flurry of attacks, just knocked down. He put his hand to where the shadow just struck him, and he was surprised to see no blood. The knight got back up and readied his own stance. I've only known this person for less than a minute, and we've already both saved each other's lives. I had come to the recognition that I had just placed myself in the middle of a fight to the death.

"Last chance. Stop this now. You won't win a two on one." The knight spoke in between breaths.

It was rather hard to tell what was racing through that shade's mind as he stood opposite to the knight and me. He gave a peculiar look at his left hand, as if surprised to see it encased in ice. He flexed it, and the ball of ice I froze around it shattered. He stretched both his arms behind him, his grip not loosening from his weapons. He tossed his head back and drew a deep breath, I could see the warm mist escaping his helmet's visor into the brisk, cold air. As he exhaled, he bent back down, and stuck his knife in the ground ready to charge at us again. His hunched over position made him look like a predatory cat. I don't think he was ready to give up and leave.

Sure enough, he propelled himself at us once more; the man's tenacity was ridiculous. His speed, agility, and intensity increased even higher than before. Now that there was an extra person to match him didn't seem to faze him at all. He struck low, bizarrely low, aiming for my legs with sweeping attacks from his great sword. Then, the next moment, he leapt overhead and swung his sword downward on the knight. I jumped over his blade and tried to freeze him mid-attack, but he was too fast. In the very same motion that he used to swing overhead with his great sword on my newfound ally, he spun to stab my side with his knife. I countered with fast growing vines, which sprung out from the ground to latch onto him. The shadow cut through. The knight parried the shadow's sword once more, the shade's grip on his dagger changed, and he switched targets, swiping it at the knight.

I fired off a jet of flame between them, separating the two, before his dagger could connect. The knight took a swing with his sword behind the fire. Alas, the shadow was no longer there. The shade darted to and fro, circling around the two of us. He kept moving, sprinting in between the trees, until he suddenly vanished again. In the instant he disappeared, he embedded his knife into the trunk, stopping his momentum in an instant. Using his embedded blade to propel him, he rapidly changed directions, spinning off the tree and aiming to cut me in two with his great sword. The knight saved me yet again by stepping in front to parry his strike. But the sheer force was enough to knock the knight into me, sending the both of us toppling over.

I got back up, and the knight did the same. Before the shadow could unleash his next flurry of moves, the knight and I reached a silent understanding. To counterattack.

The shade drew close, and I quickly unleashed my own flurry of spells. Lightning, bursts of fire, more vines, floating rocks. He dodged them all, but it kept him on his toes. I harassed him from the side, not getting between him and the knight. This forced the shade to contend with the both of us at once. The tide of battle was turning to our favor. We alternated attacks between the two of us on the man. After a short while of battling together, the knight and I got used to each other's fighting style. I matched the shadow's speed, while the knight matched his strength.

The shade tried to break off again; we didn't let that happen. As he dashed backwards into the trees, I grew a stretchy rubber sapling and wrapped it around the knight by the arm. Summoning all my strength, I threw my heavily armored ally at the shadow. I about near dislocated my shoulder with that move, especially considering that the shade already hit me hard in the same place earlier. But it was worth it. The knight let loose a substantially heavy swing. Even while off balance, the shade still somehow deflected it with his great sword. But the sheer force knocked the weapon from his hand, embedding it into the ground. I rushed forward to continue attacking, but he spun around his embedded weapon as if it were a pole in the ground and kicked me away. The knight caught me by the arm and returned my favor by throwing me at the shadow. In midair, I grabbed a nearby boulder and made it orbit me. It made several circulations around me with the split second I was airborne, increasing its speed and momentum. Then, I released it, colliding with the shade who couldn't ready his sword in time. He instead put up his arms as his defense.

The shadow was knocked back some meters away from the knight and me. Finally, a square hit. I think it was the first time the two of us even managed to touch him. After a while he got up and was bleeding. We were breathing hard, but still readied our stances for his next attacks. The shadow looked at us for ten seconds and then took his weapons and quickly left beyond the trees.

The knight, breathing hard, slowly sheathed his sword, still on guard. Then, he looked to me and pointed south, the opposite direction of the shadow. I nodded.

✎

After the rush of adrenaline that was that encounter, I started feeling the repercussions. My heartbeat loudly echoed in my eardrums, my legs felt like jelly, and I had a puking sensation that I was just able to swallow. The knight was also exhausted but seemed to handle himself much better than I could. We put some distance between the two of us and where we'd just fought, stumbling across a small clearing somewhere in the forest. Once the two of us were safe, we finally both sat down to rest. It was now nighttime.

"What was that back there?" I inquired.

"I'm not sure. That man was tracking me for some time and chose now to ambush me." The knight answered in a gruff, deep voice.

"You don't know him?"

"No."

"Then why did he attack?"

The knight shrugged. "Guess I might've upset some people I shouldn't have. Either way, I must thank you. Had you not interjected when you did, I surely wouldn't be alive right now."

"You're very welcome, although you saved me just as much. It was an honor to fight by you."

"Likewise."

The both of us kept our eyes on the tree line. Nothing came out of it. It was just the two of us and the crackling of the campfire underneath the starry sky.

"So, what made you come this way?" the knight asked.

"Ah, I'm on a project of sorts. I'm investigating Ancient ruins, and I heard there was one in the forest," I said, showing him my map.

"Hmmm? I just came from that direction." He said looking at my map. "The ruins you're looking for don't really have much left, I'm afraid. Although, there is an Ancient building on this hill here," he explained, pointing at my map. "It's some ways off from the ruins, but it is much more interesting."

"How so?"

"Well, I only saw it at a distance, but I think they built it specifically to look at the sky."

I became aware of how beautiful the sky was that night. The dim light from our campfire was not able to offset the shining stars. There was a long silence that neither of us felt the need to break. I think it was a rather nice moment I shared with this individual. It was a chance encounter that we'd become good friends in such a short amount of time.

The two of us enjoyed swapping stories to pass the time into the night. He especially got a kick out the many tales I had of Magoo. After I talked of my training, he then shared his own experiences. He was apparently an adventurer who was also in the middle of training, so to speak. Travelling the lands to hone his skill with the sword, hunting monsters, meeting with famous swordsmen, and the like. No wonder he was able to go toe to toe with that scary shadow. I could only imagine if things had gone differently, and he went after me instead.

After the two of us ran out of stories to tell, and morning came, and we both parted ways, thanking each other one more time.

Even though it may have been a foolish idea to have while that dangerous shadow might be out and about. I ended up going back into the forest, wanting to see the building the knight described. I was hopeful in thinking that the shadow wouldn't expect me to return into the forest, and thankfully, I didn't see him. Coming across another small clearing with a steep hill in the middle of the forest, I saw the Ancient building in question. It was strange, even by the Ancient's standards.

It was a cylindrical structure, with an incredibly smooth dome on its top. Although the building was deteriorating enough to see cracks upon its surface, it was for the most part intact. On top of the dome was an opening with another cylinder poking out of it, aiming straight up to the sky, and it was tipped with glass.

I entered the building fascinated by what I found. Texts of the Ancients, describing their sciences, chemistry, physics, biology, and all. It would take many days in order to copy it all down. Exactly what Magoo sent me to look for. And I figured out what the building was made for; it was a telescope. In the early moments of that morning, I enjoyed watching the stars.

Chapter Twenty-Four
The Puppet Master

AFTER DOING ODD QUESTS, SEARCHING FOR ANCIENT RUINS, and sparring against all manners of creatures, I returned to Angrost in exactly one year's time. I spent the entire time researching what I've learned from the Ancient's teachings, and I thought I accomplished what my teacher sent me out to do. I still don't know if I am anywhere close to creating an Apocalyptic spell, but I have worked on my magic enough for it to be a force to be reckoned with. Hopefully if I ever saw that shadow again, I'd be ready.

Along the path to the capital, I spotted a familiar face heading in the same direction as mine. It was Old Man Magoo. He was carrying something wrapped up on his back as he walked, making him look even more hunched over than usual, which was a feat in and of itself.

"Hi, Magoo."

"Whointhegoshdarnflippingscallopsareyou?"

Did he just call me a scallop?

"Oh, it's just you kid." Magoo regained his breath.

"So, what's that you're carrying?"

"Oh this," he said pointing to his back. "It's something of a surprise of sorts, don't wanna ruin it."

"Then why don't you just keep it in your shack?"

Magoo grinned. "It won't fit! Or should I say the material it's made out of won't shrink. You ain't the only one whose been busy this year youngin'! Anyway, it will take some time to get it ready for you in the shack. You take this time to see your folks again."

I nodded. I couldn't help but notice that he put the shack closer to Angrost than the time I first met him.

⌒

I entered the gates to the capital and proceeded down the streets to the house where I used to live. For the most part, the area was much quieter than I remember, and there seemed to be less people. That was until I caught the scent of heavy smoke in the air and looked up. In the sky, I saw a plume of black smoke, emanating from the direction of my home. I started running. When I reached my destination, I was met with the worst sight I could imagine. My family's house, which had deteriorated over time and was already in shambles, was now on fire. Everyone in our neighborhood was in a panic as I stood agape at the burning house in front of me. Behind me, I could hear a thud of someone dropping their things, my father's expression was the same as mine; miserable disbelief. I had not been home in over three years, and this was the way we met.

"Your . . . mother . . . is . . ." He could barely speak beyond a whisper. "Lisandra? LISANDRA!" My father shouted at the top of his lungs and rushed into the burning building.

"No! Don't—" There was no use in screaming after him. He went after my mother, regardless of my pleas. I needed to think fast. The only thing that came to mind was how Magoo put out the fires in the Rotten Forest.

I mimicked his movements and pointed at the clouds. To my surprise, it somehow worked, and the steady rain fall extinguished the fires to my home. But the smoke only cleared to show me a worse sight engraved in my memory. It was of Isaac, my father,

150

holding the crisp remains of my dead mother. Her body was burnt to a husk and her face was charred. My throat dried, and I couldn't swallow. Of the thoughts and emotions that swam round my head, inevitable truths were presented before me now whether I wanted to accept them or not. My mother was dead. And I would never see her again. And that thought hurt harder than any blow I'd ever taken before.

"Lisa . . . ndra," Isaac croaked.

Together, we both broke down and cried till dusk.

The funeral we had for her was depressingly brief. Only my dad and I showed up, with Magoo observing somewhere off to the side. The rain I had summoned the day before only grew, making the weather over Angrost gloomier than usual. Memories ran by me. Moments when my mother cared for me, moments when she hugged me warmly. So many moments that would never be relived again. My throat stiffened with grief.

Despite my many pleas for him not to return to the court of Pravah, Isaac did so anyway the next day. He left me with the words "Be strong, and live." Like he'd never see me again.

With nowhere else to go, I moved back into Magoo's shack. This time, Matthew didn't fight me back and opened the door for me. The words on him did not read "not-welcome" anymore, and the Venus fly-trap didn't try to bite me that day. I ventured in and sat down in front of Magoo, who was waiting for me.

"It's such a shame. Losing someone that close to you is hardest pain I can think of. What's worse is that I believe there will be more pain to come." We both stared at each other in silence for an agonizingly long time.

"I've been thinking about it," Magoo continued. "I want you to be my successor, the new grandmaster mage. I think it's probably the best future for you now. Surely, you know what that means . . ."

"I have to defeat you?"

"No." Magoo looked at me with a serious expression. "You must kill me."

"No, I'm not going to—I *can't* kill my mentor." I sobbed. I wanted him to stop talking. This wasn't the end. I relied so much on his advice, and he'd given me so much. The last thing I wanted was for him to leave me too.

"I am old and sick and going to die anyway. The only way you will get my title is by ending my life. And that will give you standing in this nation. You must become the grandmaster to save Pravah from its own nobility. Yes, even a hermit like me can see when chaos begins to brew. Only problem is, I'm too damn old to do anything about it. So, as unfair as it may be, the duty of what's to come will fall upon you. If you don't want your father to join your mother, then kill me." The look he gave me was one to remember, it was if he was pleading with me to end his life. At that moment, Magoo's age became much more apparent to me. His wrinkles were numerous, and his face sagged. He coughed.

Didn't he always have a bad cough throughout my training?

"Know this, boy: the life of a grandmaster mage requires you to step as far as you can from humanity. You saw firsthand just how grotesque our trade is. My blood-soaked hands are a reminder to me every day that this is the way I live, and you will be the same as me. It's what we both have chosen. I want you to have the power I couldn't and make our field of work into a noble one. End my life," Magoo commanded.

"NO! I will not trade YOUR life for my father's!" I stormed out of his shack before he could say another word.

This was at a time before we had tournaments. The only way the public acknowledged the change in grandmasters was from the death of the original. In order for me to become a grandmaster myself, I had to kill Magoo. Instead of facing the difficult choice I had to make, I decided to hide, shying away from everyone with self-pity.

My indecisiveness would only get me into more trouble. I decided that my father would know what to do. He and the last few nobles still loyal to the King were rumored to be meeting together. Their issue to be discussed was the possible uprising of rebellion. Their meeting took too long, but I had no clue where it could be in Angrost. With the house burned down, there was no other place that I could think of where they might hold that meeting. I had to search in the courtroom to try and find anything. Distrusting the noblemen around him, Isaac used to hide his notes in a locked box under the floorboards of the courtroom's cellar; there was no way to pry them open without getting some attention.

I arrived in the courtroom in a state of disbelief. All the people who worked there were either gone or killed. The floorboards were smashed open, and so was the locked box that held the location of Isaac's meeting: a loyal noble's house in the city. Not bothering to report the crime, I left at once for the nobleman's home.

Hurrying to house, I opened the door to find a bloodbath. The noblemen were assassinated. Each one of them had knives in a vital spot, very professionally done. None of this was hidden from sight, it was almost like the assassin wanted people to find the bodies.

The last of the dead noblemen I saw was my father. I would have cried if I had any tears left in me. Instead, I just stared at his corpse. I felt only regret for not helping my parents sooner.

⤜⤛

The funeral that was held for my father was just as short and brief as it was for my mother. This time, it was just me standing before his fresh dug grave. I had no tears left to shed. The weather was insultingly sunny and beautiful after the rainfall I caused.

On my walk back into the city, I was blocked by Magoo standing at Angrost's gates, along with a small crowd.

"It's time," he said.

I was silent.

"There is only one way you can graduate as my student, and that is by replacing me." Magoo coughed.

I was silent.

Magoo fired a bolt of purple light that narrowly missed me. I just looked back at him with dead eyes.

"I know I ask much of you, but when you're at your worse is exactly when I need you to try your best. For your sake, more than anyone else's. I know you fear losing me, someone you rely on. But death is a very normal aspect of life. The two are synonymous. So, in a way, it is nothing to fear as we continue to pass. Just the same way as we pass on what we've learned to our descendants. Which is where I stand before you now." He fired more bolts of purple light. This time, they hit me.

I slowly staggered backwards, still silent.

"Damnit, boy! Fight back! Now is not the time to give up! Now is not the time to surrender!" Magoo coughed again, then sighed. "You and I both know how this fight ends. You may not want it, you may even despise it, but you will take my title. With it you can do more than you've ever imagined, because that is exactly where the limits of magic itself lie, your imagination!"

Magoo coughed again. "So, pick yourself up! Dust yourself off! Scream with ALL the rage in your heart! Find your own future and fight for it! Stretch your creativity as far as you can go, for that's what it truly means to do the unthinkable." He fired again.

I finally listened to him, I grew a small sapling and blocked the spell. It was the last advice given to me by my teacher who I chose to follow. I let go of the sadness I felt and embraced my fury. I got mad. Mad that my mother was gone. Mad that father is gone. Mad that Magoo will soon be gone. I embraced the resolve that I would find the ones responsible for all of this. My targets were Count Montegew and Duke Jeffery. The look in my eyes was no longer dead.

"That's more like it." Magoo looked proud. "I, Magoo Stoneheart the Puppet Master, Grandmaster Mage, challenge Franklin Olsenhein to trial by combat."

He put both hands to the ground and raised both of them as puppeteering hands. Before him, an army made of stone began to assemble. They looked nothing like the mannequins I've fought before. They seemed more sturdily constructed, as if the thicker rock midsections gave off the appearance of armor. Most of them carried large shields also made of stone, and sharpened granite in their hands to make up their swords and spears. The rest just had rocks with slings. What's more, there was twice as much to contend with thanks to Magoo's second puppeteering hand.

I started off trying the same strategy as before, slip past them to get to Magoo. The first one of them didn't let me. He instantly slammed into me with his shield, propelling me a couple of meters. Immediately after, the ones with slings pelted me with their rocks. I dodged, but not quickly enough. One of them managed to strike me in the ribs. I looked down at the stone that hit me. It was shaped like a clutched fist. Before I had just Magoo to keep an eye on when he tried to snipe at me. Now, there was a whole mess of ranged opponents hiding amongst the crowd made of stone that was slowly surrounding me. The ones with spears formed a phalanx and a tight shield wall, gradually advancing me. The ones with swords cut off my retreat and plugged any holes in their lines. These mannequins could put trained soldiers to shame.

Dodging them all was not an option, beating them all one by one was even less so. To defeat Magoo I needed a spell of my own creation, something that I've learned on my own, my own magic. After backing away from Magoo's forces, I've achieved one second in order to concentrate. The air around me grew dense and cold, I dashed forward, like a spring held back taunt, through the phalanx made of stone, freezing every mannequin in front of me in an instant. It was a frost flash, a chilled straight line of blue that ended with my hand placed directly upon Magoo. I froze him solid and watched his smiling face crumble away to dust just the same as his creations. I made sure the spell I used was as quick and painless as possible, for it was the only thing I could give back to the teacher who gave me the most.

Forced to kill my mentor and witness the death of everyone I knew, through great hardship, I was granted the rank of grandmaster mage. I still felt like the cost was too great, and all of this was for nothing.

⤳

I went back to last home I knew: Magoo's shack. There was none of the life I was once greeted with when I first arrived. The giant Venus flytrap was wilted away and was dried up. Matthew didn't greet me this time; he was as expressionless as a regular doormat. Inside the shack, all of Magoo's experiments were finished. No more potions, and the vials were emptied. Essentially nothing was left, save for one thing on the rickety table in the center of the shack.

It was a metallic staff, the same one I carry to this day, and around it was wrapped a parchment. I unwrapped the parchment from the staff and found not only words from Magoo, but also my father's penmanship.

The note from Magoo only read, "I've said what I needed to say. Rest is up to you."

It gave me a sad chuckle. That would be just like him.

The other note was from my father.

Dear Frank,

This letter holds my last words to you that I place in the care of your teacher. My son, it hurts me to know that my death is imminent, and that I shamefully leave you to better serve our nation. My greatest regret I have ever had is leaving you alone. I could not protect your mother, nor can I protect you, but with the little we have left, I can give you the means to protect yourself. Magoo pitched in enough money and time to create this staff for you to practice your love of magic. He says it is special, and one of a kind. And what is more, I could tell he really means it, which is why it is all the more prefect for you. We can tell, that if you practice hard and train even harder, you'll be able to do anything! Know that wherever you go, wherever you may be, your mother and I love you very much.

My tears found their way back to me.

Chapter Twenty-Five
An Unlikely Alliance

AFTER SPENDING SOME TIME ALONE, I LEFT THE SHACK. Leaving behind more bitter memories than I care to remember, I sought to seek council with the only person I knew left who wouldn't try to kill me, the King himself. I visited the inner castle keep of Angrost.

The halls were empty. What used to hold many squabbling nobles debating amongst themselves now had only a few mice squeaking about. My footsteps echoed quite loudly in the empty rooms leading up to the King. He only had two guards on either side of me and allowed me to approach him.

"You, you're Isaac's boy, aren't you?" said Reginold.

"Yes, sir."

"Such a shame, losing someone that talented. He was the best we had. I will sorely miss him."

"Yes, sir."

"You just recently became the new grandmaster mage, correct?"

"Yes, sir."

The King got out of his chair and approached me, face to face. "So, what are you going to do now?"

It was a good question, one that I didn't really know the answer to.

"Do you blame me for Isaac's death? Is that it? You came here to avenge your mother and father?" When the King said this, the guards next to him aimed their spears at me, but he waved them down.

"No, sir. That is unless you are the one who killed him . . ." The first threat I make to anyone, and I stupidly made it against the King of my own country. Not only that, but those were the first words I spoke to the King other than "yes sir." I wished I could sew my mouth shut at that point.

King Reginold was solemn. "Yes, I can see why you say that. Instead of giving him better protection, I decided to put my trust in Montegew and Jeffrey, only to get stabbed in the back. Isaac was right, I could only find out the truth when it didn't even matter anymore. There were eyewitness reports that placed Montegew at that incident with the hospital, but I could only find out later that Duke Jefferey halted those testimonies from ever getting into the court. I'm going to level with you kid. We've got a civil war on our hands. Those two are gathering forces to march on me, and," he looked all around his deserted halls, "I don't have the manpower to fight them."

"So, then you want me to help?" I asked.

"Yes, but I will need more than just one kid. Even if you are a grandmaster."

"Then I will find a way to get more men."

The King gave me a peculiar look. "Why are you doing this?" I was silent.

"You want to find them, don't you? The ones who took your parents——"

"I will depart immediately to recruit reinforcements." I cut off his sentence.

"Very well." The King grumbled. "I give you my good grace to go out into the world. I will delegate you as an emissary for the time being. But know this, I cannot help you in the slightest. Even though you gain my enemies, you will not gain my aid."

"Yes, sir." I was getting used to working alone.

I left the castle, and started to wander . . .

Chapter Twenty-Six
The Tale Continues

F RANK'S STORY LEFT HIS AUDIENCE SILENT.
There was a mix of emotions that no one knew what exactly to
convey. Whether it was shock, disbelief, or to try and console him,
neither Revina, Serge, nor Isabelle attempted to provide their input
in fear of hurting Frank's sentiments.

"That . . . was very detailed," Serge spoke up.

Isabelle punched his shoulder.

"Ow, what?"

"You're being insensitive."

He sighed, "Yeah, sorry. But I think I'm about to be even more
insensitive. Frank, even though I very much appreciate you sharing
your childhood with us, you still haven't answered my most
pressing questions. I understand you're trying to give us your
background, and I am grateful you're finally opening up to us. It
gives me an opportunity to learn about you, which is a big reason
why we started this conversation in the first place. But . . . we still
need to know. Who were the Elites? And what happened during
the Dark Crisis? I can't help but feel like the part in this tale that
comes next . . . you're trying to avoid."

More silence.

"Yeah," Frank rasped. "Maybe I kinda have."

"Frank . . ." Revina started. She looked like there was much she wanted to say, but just decided on one thing. "Do you remember that first spell you tried to teach me?"

"The healing spell."

"Isn't it the same as . . . ?"

"Yes."

Revina had a worried complexion. "Back at the graves where I found you . . . I tried that spell. I could've—I could've . . ."

"Yes."

Revina became downcast. She buried her head in her arms in shame. "I'm so sorry." She felt terrible, frustrated that all she could offer was a cheap apology.

"It's not on you to apologize at all." Frank put a reassuring hand on her shoulder. "It's my fault. I didn't have the heart to . . . teach you properly." He looked to Serge. "Much like how I didn't have the courage say everything I could. I'd like to think I've grown a little since meeting you two. And seeing the both of you still keep your faith in me, even after all that's happened, well . . . I appreciate it. Greatly."

Revina looked up, feeling slightly better.

Frank inhaled deeply. "I'm ready. To tell you the rest. There's still much that remains to be said. Much that remains to be remembered. Much to think about. These stories tell the past of those I once knew, and those I cared to never remember again. So, gather around and listen closely. To fate of a kingdom, the fate of people, and the fate of myself. The tales of a wanderer."